Adventures of UNCLE WIGGILY

Howard Garis

with Illustrations by Louis Wisa

DOVER PUBLICATIONS, INC.
Mineola, New York

Bibliographical Note

This Dover edition, first published in 2008, is a new selection of stories from the following works by Howard R. Garis: *Sammie and Susie Littletail,* A. L. Burt Company, New York, 1910; *Uncle Wiggily's Adventures,* A. L. Burt Company, New York, 1912; *Uncle Wiggily's Fortune,* A. L. Burt Company, New York, 1913; and *Uncle Wiggily's Travels,* A. L. Burt Company, New York, 1913. Some of the stories have been slightly edited for continuity. The original illustrations by Louis Wisa have been specially colored for the Dover edition.

Library of Congress Cataloging-in-Publication Data

Garis, Howard Roger, 1873–1962.
     Adventures of Uncle Wiggily / Howard R. Garis ; with illustrations by Louis Wisa.
        p. cm.
     "A new selection of stories from the following works by Howard R. Garis: *Sammie and Susie Littletail,* A. L. Burt Company, New York, 1910; *Uncle Wiggily's Adventures,* A. L. Burt Company, New York, 1912; *Uncle Wiggily's Fortune,* A. L. Burt Company, New York, 1913; and *Uncle Wiggily's Travels,* A. L. Burt Company, New York, 1913."
     Summary: A collection of stories about the adventures of a wise rabbit and his animal and human friends.
     ISBN-13: 978-0-486-46028-4
     ISBN-10: 0-486-46028-2
       1. Children's stories, American. [1. Rabbits—Fiction. 2. Animals—Fiction. 3. Short stories.] I. Wisa, Louis, ill. II. Title.

PZ7.G182Adv 2008
[Fic]—dc22

                                                                                    2007050545

Manufactured in China
Dover Publications, Inc., 31 East 2nd Street, Mineola, N.Y. 11501

CONTENTS

UNCLE WIGGILY AND THE FOX

Once upon a time, not so very many years ago, there lived an old gentleman rabbit named Uncle Wiggily Longears. He was a nice, quiet sort of a bunny, and he had lots of friends among other rabbits, and squirrels, and ducks, and doggies, and pussy cats, and mice and lambs, and all sorts of animals.

Most especially there was a muskrat lady, named Miss Jane Fuzzy-Wuzzy, who liked Uncle Wiggily very much. She made a crutch for him, when he had the rheumatism. She gnawed it out of a cornstalk for him, and painted it red, white and blue with raspberry jam.

Well, Uncle Wiggily was a funny old rabbit gentleman. He was always having adventures—which means things happening to you, such as stubbing your toe, or getting lost or things like that. He traveled all around looking for his fortune, so he would be rich. But he didn't find it for some time, though many things happened to him.

The last thing that happened was that he tore his nice coat, and a good tailor bird kindly mended it for him. And he stayed at her house for some time, bringing up coal, and sweeping the sidewalk, and things like that to be useful; for Uncle Wiggily was very kind.

He used to sleep in a hollow stump, near the nest of the tailor bird, and one night it rained so hard that he had to go to bed and pull the dried leaves up over him to keep warm. All night it rained, and in the morning Uncle Wiggily got up, and he was hoping it had cleared off, so he could travel on and seek his fortune, and get rich.

Out of bed hopped Uncle Wiggily. In one corner of the stump was his valise in which he carried his lunch and clean clothes and the like of that.

The day before, a bad wolf had chased Uncle Wiggily, catching him and tearing his coat, so that now the rabbit gentleman was quite stiff and sore. Still he managed to move about.

"Oh, dear me!" he exclaimed as he looked out of a hole in the stump, and saw the big rain drops still pattering down, "this is a very poor day for me to find my fortune. Still, I can't stay in on account of the weather, so I will get my breakfast and travel on."

He had some carrot and lettuce sandwiches in his valise and he ate these and then looked out to see if the rain had stopped, but it had not, I am sorry to say.

"Well," Uncle Wiggily said. "I don't like to get wet, but there is no help for it. I'll start out." Then he happened to think of something. "I know what I'll do!" he exclaimed. "I'll get the largest toadstool I can find, and use it for an umbrella."

Out he ran and soon he had picked a big toadstool that made as fine an umbrella as one could wish. Then, strapping his satchel to his back, where it would be out of the way, the old gentleman rabbit hopped off, holding the toadstool umbrella over his head, and limping along on his barberpole crutch. And as he went over the meadows and through the woods he sang this little song, and sometimes when one sings it just at the right time, why it stops raining almost at once. But it has to be sung at the proper time. Anyhow this is the song:

>"Splish-splash! Drip-dash!
> How the raindrops fall!
> When the weather gets too wet,
> It isn't nice at all.

>"Mr. Rain, oh, please go 'way!
> For my feet are wet.
> And you're splashing on my nose.
> What? You can't stop yet?

"Won't you please be nice to me—
Make your raindrops dry.
I am sure you could do this
If you'd only try.

"Dry raindrops are very nice,
And if they would fall,
We could walk in showers, and
Not get wet at all."

Well, as soon as Uncle Wiggily had sung this song, he looked up quickly from under his toadstool umbrella to see if it had stopped raining, but it hadn't, and he got a drop right in his left eye, which made him sneeze so hard that his spectacles fell off. And they dropped right into a mud puddle.

"Ha, hum!" exclaimed the old gentleman rabbit, "this is a pretty kettle of fish!" Of course, he didn't mean that there was a kettle of fish in the mud puddle, but that was his manner of talking, because he was so surprised. "A very pretty kettle of fish, indeed!" cried the old gentleman rabbit, "and speaking of fish, I guess I'll have to fish for my spectacles."

So what did he do but use his red-white-and-blue-striped-barber-pole crutch for a fishing pole, and he dipped it down in the mud puddle and in a little while up came his glasses wiggling on the end of the crutch just like an eel.

"That is good luck!" said the rabbit, as he wiped off the mud and water and put on his spectacles, and he was just going to put his toadstool umbrella over his head again when he found out that the rain had stopped and he didn't need it.

Then he left the toadstool hanging on a berry bush by the mud puddle to dry, so that whoever came along next time would have an umbrella all ready for the rain.

"Well, now that the sun is coming out I must be on the watch for my fortune," said the old gentleman rabbit to himself. And he peered first on one side of the road and then on the other, but not a sign of his fortune could he see.

Then, all of a sudden he saw something shining golden yellow in a field close by.

"Ah, that must be a pile of yellow gold!" exclaimed Uncle Wiggily. "Now my fortune is made!" and he hopped over to the field. But alas! and alack-a-day! Instead of being gold the pile of yellow things were carrots.

"Well, it might be worse!" said the rabbit. "At least I can eat carrots. I wonder if whoever they belong to would mind if I took some?"

"I wouldn't mind a bit!" exclaimed a voice. "Take as many as you like, Uncle Wiggily," and up jumped Mr. Groundhog, who owned the carrots. "Take all you can eat and fill your valise," said Mr. Groundhog.

"Thank you very kindly," replied the rabbit, so he ate several carrots and filled his satchel with more, and then he and Mr. Groundhog talked about the weather, and things like that, until it was time for Uncle Wiggily to hop on again after his fortune.

But he didn't find it, and pretty soon it came on toward night, and the old gentleman rabbit looked for a place to stay while it was dark.

"I think this will do," he said, when he came to a small stone cave. "I'll just crawl in here with my carrots and my crutch," and in he crawled as nicely as a basket of shavings.

Pretty soon Uncle Wiggily was fast, fast asleep, and he never thought the least mite about any danger. But danger was close at hand just the same.

Hark! What's that creeping, creeping along under the bushes? Eh? What's that? Why, my goodness me sakes alive and a piece of pie! It's the fuzzy old fox! Yes, as true as I'm telling you, the old red fox had seen Uncle Wiggily go into the cave, and now he was snooping and snipping up to catch him if he could.

"Oh, I'll soon have a fine time!" said the fox in a whisper, smacking his lips. Into the cave he crawled, and in the darkness he happened to knock over Uncle Wiggily's crutch, which was standing in a corner. Quickly the old gentleman rabbit awakened when he heard the noise. Up he jumped and he cried out:

"Who's there?"

"I'm the fox," was the answer, "and I came to catch you."

But do you s'pose Uncle Wiggily was afraid? Not a bit of it. He ran to his valise and he took out a pawful of carrots with their sharp points, and before that fox could even sneeze the rabbit threw one carrot at him and hit him on the nose, for Uncle Wiggily could see in the dark.

Then he threw another carrot and hit the fox on the ear, and then he threw still another one and he hit him on the two eyes, and that fox was so frightened and surprised that he jumped out of the second-story window of the cave house and sprained his toenail. Then he ran back to his den and didn't bother Uncle Wiggily any more that night, and the rabbit slept in peace and quietness, and dreamed about Santa Claus and ice-cream popcorn balls.

UNCLE WIGGILY AND THE MONKEY

Uncle Wiggily, with Peetie and Jackie Bow-Wow, was walking along the road toward the puppy dogs' grandpa's house, and they were talking how Jackie had made the black bear run away by pointing a make-believe wooden gun at the savage creature. All at once the old gentleman rabbit exclaimed:

"That grasshopper!"

"What about the grasshopper?" asked Jackie. "Did one bite you, Uncle Wiggily?"

"No, but my friend, the green grasshopper, jumped into a Jack-in-the-Pulpit when the bear came, and here we have come away and forgotten all about him. We must go right back."

So back they started, and on the way the rabbit told what a kind friend the grasshopper had been to him on his travels. Well, they got to the place where the bear had scared them, but when they looked up on the rock no Jack-in-the-Pulpit was to be seen, and there was no sign of the grasshopper.

"I'm sure it was here that the grasshopper made his jump," said Uncle Wiggily, looking carefully about.

"Yes," said Jackie, "but there is no Jack-in-the-Pulpit on this rock at all."

"Here is a pile of dirt, though," spoke Peetie. "Perhaps there is a bone under it. Let's dig, Jackie."

So those two puppy dogs dug in the earth while Uncle Wiggily looked all around for the grasshopper. Then, all of a sudden, Peetie cried out:

"Oh! Look here! The Jack-in-the-Pulpit is under this pile of earth! The top is just sticking out. Now, we'll find the hoppergrass."

"I see how it is," said the rabbit. "When the bear ran away so fast from Jackie's wooden gun the toenails of the savage creature scattered up the earth, and it went in a shower all over the Jack where the grasshopper was hidden. No wonder we couldn't find him, for he was buried. But please dig very carefully, Peetie and Jackie, or you might scratch him with your paws."

"We will be careful," said Jackie. So he and his brother dug and dug, until the Jack-in-the-Pulpit was almost uncovered. Then they didn't dig any more, but, with their tails, which were like dusting brushes, they dashed off the earth very gently, until the plant was all clear, and out popped the grasshopper, not a bit harmed, though he was somewhat frightened.

"My! I thought I'd never get out!" exclaimed the jumping chap, taking a long breath, and blowing the dust off his legs.

Then he was introduced to Jackie Bow-Wow, whom he had not met before, and the four friends trudged along the road together. Pretty soon they came to the house of Grandpa Bark, and the old gentleman dog was very glad to see Peetie, who had been lost, and had stayed away all night.

"And I am very glad to see you also, Uncle Wiggily," said Grandpa Bark, "and likewise the grasshopper. Come in and have something to eat, and stay awhile to rest yourself."

So Uncle Wiggily did this, and after a bit he said:

"Well, now, I must be off once more to seek my fortune. When I find it I am going back home, and I hope that soon comes to pass, for I am tired of traveling about."

So he said good-by to Peetie and Jackie Bow-Wow, and he and the grasshopper hopped off together. On and on they went, over the hills and dales, through the woods and fields, and pretty soon they came to a place in the woods where there was a big box. It was almost as large as a small house, and it had a front door to it, but no windows. The front door was open and over it was a card reading:

"COME IN, IF YOU WANT TO."

"Ha, hum! I wonder if that means me?" said Uncle Wiggily. "Perhaps I may find my fortune in there. I'm going inside."

"I wouldn't if I were you," spoke the grasshopper. "It may be a trap."

"Nonsensicalness!" exclaimed the old gentleman rabbit, quick-like. "Come along. We'll go in."

So he and the grasshopper went inside, but no sooner had they entered, than slam-bang! down came the sliding door with a crash, catching them fast there just like mice in a trap.

"Oh, what did I tell you!" cried the grasshopper, sadly. "This is a trap! We're in it."

"Yes, I see we are," spoke Uncle Wiggily, much puzzled. "It was all my fault. I should have been more careful."

"Never mind," said the grasshopper, kindly, as he wiped away his tears on a piece of green leaf. "I see a crack between the boards that I can crawl through. It is too small for you, but I can get out, and I'll go for help."

So out he crawled, leaving Uncle Wiggily there. The old gentleman rabbit was thinking of the dreadful things that might happen to him, when, all of a sudden, he heard some one unlocking the front door that had fallen shut.

"I must see who that is!" whispered the rabbit to himself. So he peered out of a crack, and he saw something red and fuzzy-like at the door. "Oh, it's a red bear!" thought the rabbit, and he was looking for a place to hide, when all at once the door opened and there stood a nice, kind red monkey, with a red cap on.

"Oh, I've got company, I see!" cried the red monkey in delight. "I'm glad of that, Uncle Wiggily. I've been waiting some time to see you. How did you get here?"

"Isn't—isn't this a trap?" asked the rabbit.

"Not a bit of it!" cried the red monkey with a jolly laugh. "This is my house. I went out this morning and left the door open. It must have blown shut by mistake. I'm sorry you were frightened. Wait, I'll do some tricks to make you laugh."

So the red monkey stood on his nose, and then on one ear,

and then he made all the letters of the alphabet on his tail, all except the letter "X," which is very hard for a monkey to make. Then the monkey took two apple pies and made them into one, and he and Uncle Wiggily ate it, and my! how good it was. By this time the rabbit wasn't frightened any more, and he told the red monkey all about his travels to find a fortune. And then the grasshopper came hopping back with Old Dog Percival to help Uncle Wiggily get out of the trap, but there wasn't any need, for it was no trap at all, you see.

So the red monkey and the dog and the grasshopper and the old gentleman rabbit had a nice time at the house of the red monkey, who told them many stories.

UNCLE WIGGILY AND THE WATERMELON

"Well," asked the slow snail of Uncle Wiggily, as he met the old gentleman rabbit on the beach one day, "did you get any of your fortune at the fleas' party?"

"None at all," answered the old gentleman rabbit. "There was plenty of gold and diamonds to be seen, but the fleas didn't give me any."

"Perhaps they forgot it?" suggested the snail. "Some of the fleas are very forgetful. I once knew one whose mother sent him to the store for a pound of sugar and a quart of milk, and what do you s'pose he bought?"

"I don't know," answered the rabbit, curious-like.

"He got a pound of milk and a quart of sugar, and the milk all ran out of the paper bag in which the groceryman put it, and the sugar stuck fast to the milk pail, and they had a dreadful time getting it out. That shows you what a flea will do sometimes. Perhaps if you ask them for your fortune they will give it to you."

"I'll do it the next time I meet one," decided Uncle Wiggily. "But now I must go on and look for myself."

"Wait until I sing a little song for you," said the slow snail, and he hummed this song very, very slowly:

> "When I am in a hurry
> I slowly crawl along,
> And when I finish crawling
> I sing a little song.

> "For if I hurried too much
> I'd get there all too soon,
> Though some day I am going
> To climb up to the moon.

"And then when I get up there
I'll sleep the whole long day,
Or crawl upon the moonbeams,
Or jump into the hay."

"Ha! hum!" exclaimed Uncle Wiggily. "That's a very good song, and I'm sure it will help me find my fortune. Now I must say good-by and travel along."

"If you will wait I'll come with you," spoke the snail. "But then I s'pose you are in a hurry, Uncle Wiggily, and I go too slow for you."

"That's it," said the rabbit kindly, and he gave one big hop that carried him twice as far as the snail could travel in a week of Sundays without counting Christmas.

Well, it wasn't very long after this before Uncle Wiggily got to the top of a hill. When he started to climb up from the bottom he thought perhaps there might be gold at the top, but when he did get to the summit all he found there was a big green thing, with stripes on.

"I wonder what this can be?" thought the rabbit. "It looks like a baseball, and yet it's too large for that, and besides it isn't quite round. And, once more, it's green instead of white, for all baseballs are white. Ha! I know what it is. That must be a football which the boys kick about. I guess I'll kick it. Perhaps there may be gold inside."

So he got ready to kick it, but you know how it is with old gentlemen rabbits who have the rheumatism and have to go about on a crutch. As soon as Uncle Wiggily lifted up one foot—the one that had no rheumatism in it—and when he leaned on his crutch, the crutch suddenly slipped, and down he went ker-flumux ker-flimix all in a heap.

"Well, here's a pretty kettle of fish!" he cried. "I ought never to have tried to kick that green football. I should have waited until it was ripe."

So he sat down on top of the hill, and looked at the ocean tumbling and foaming on the beach below him, and he waited for the green football to get ripe. And, every once in a while he would poke it with his crutch to see if it was getting soft, but it wasn't.

And once, right after he did this, the old gentleman rabbit heard some one cry out:

"My goodness, Uncle Wiggily! What are you doing?"

"Waiting for this green football to get ripe so that I can kick it," was the rabbit's reply.

"Oh, ho! Oh, ha!" laughed the grasshopper, for it was that leaping insect who had spoken, "that is not a football, it is a watermelon, and inside it is all red and sweet and juicy. Come, if you can, cut it open, we will have a fine feast. I haven't had any watermelon in some time. Can you cut it?"

"Oh, I can cut it fast enough," declared the rabbit. "Here goes, and I hope it is better looking on the inside than it is on the outside."

So the rabbit took out his knife, with which he usually spread his bread and butter, and he cut a hole in the watermelon. Then Uncle Wiggily and the grasshopper scooped out all the nice, red, juicy part and ate it.

And, would you ever believe it? Something happened right after that. They had no sooner wiped the red watermelon juice off their faces than there was a terrible roaring sound in the bushes, and out jumped a big black bear. Oh, he was going on something frightful, yes, really he was, but don't be frightened, for I won't let him hurt anybody. I'll let him chew on my typewriter first and that will dull his teeth. On the bear came, straight for the watermelon.

"Oh, what can I do?" cried Uncle Wiggily. "That bear will get me, but he won't hurt you, Mr. Grasshopper, as you are so small."

"Don't worry," said the hoppergrass, kindly. "I'll find a way to save you. Quick! Before the bear sees you, hop inside the watermelon," for you see they had eaten up all the inside, and left the melon rind hollow, just like a yellow pumpkin Jack-o'-lantern, at Hallowe'en.

Uncle Wiggily saw that this was the best thing to do, so inside the melon he hopped, and then the grasshopper put back in place the piece they had cut out, and you never would have known but that the melon was a whole, new one, never having been cut and the inside eaten out.

On came the bear, sniffing with his black nose. Then he saw the grasshopper and asked, suspicious-like:

"Is there a rabbit around here?"

"I don't see any," spoke the grasshopper, and he really couldn't see any one but the bear because Uncle Wiggily was inside the melon, you know.

"Well, if there is no rabbit I'll have to eat this watermelon, then," said the bear, "for I am very hungry."

Now the grasshopper knew that if the bear once bit into the melon and opened it, he'd see the rabbit hiding inside. So what did the hoppergrass do but give the melon a shove with his strong hind legs, and down the hill the melon rolled, with the rabbit in it, just as Buddy Pigg, the guinea pig boy, once rolled down hill inside a cabbage.

Faster and faster down the hill rolled the melon, with Uncle Wiggily in it, and then the bear saw one of the rabbit's paws sticking out of a crack.

"Oh, ho! You have fooled me!" cried the bear to the grasshopper. "Now, I'll chase after that melon and get the rabbit, too!"

So the bear started down the hill after the melon, but his foot slipped and he slid down, oh, so fast, that he got to the bottom of the hill first. There he stood waiting for Uncle Wiggily. But a queer thing happened. The melon hit a stone, burst open and out flew the rabbit on a pile of soft sand. But the pieces of the melon hit the bear on his soft and tender nose, and he thought he was surely killed, and off he ran to the woods howling and growling. So that's how Uncle Wiggily escaped from the bear, for the old gentleman rabbit wasn't hurt a bit for all his tumble.

Then he washed the pieces of melon off his clothes, and traveled on again, with the grasshopper, to seek his fortune.

UNCLE WIGGILY AND THE WORMS

"Well, where in the world have you been?" asked the red monkey of Uncle Wiggily, as the old gentleman rabbit hopped along after he had gotten out of the molasses can.

"Oh, I had an adventure," replied the rabbit, and he told how a hippity-hop toad had saved him from the sticky stuff. "But can you whistle yet, red monkey?" asked Uncle Wiggily.

"No, he doesn't seem to be able to do it," spoke the green parrot, in a sort of sad and hopeless tone. "Every time he tries to whistle he puckers his face up in such a funny way that I have to laugh, and when I laugh I can't whistle. Can't you keep your face straight, so I won't have to giggle?" asked the green bird, solemnlike.

"I can't seem to," replied the monkey, and he made another effort to whistle, but he puckered up such a funny face, and his tail got all tied up in a hard knot, and he looked so queer that even Uncle Wiggily had to laugh.

"You see how it is," said the parrot. "I can't give whistling lessons and laugh at the same time," and then he had to laugh. "Ha! Ha!" and "Ho! Ho!" because you see the monkey made another queer face trying to get the knots out of his tail.

"I think I have a plan," said Uncle Wiggily after a bit.

"What is it?" asked the monkey.

"You must get behind a tree, red monkey," said the rabbit. "Then the parrot can tell you how to whistle, and give you a lesson without seeing the funny faces you make. Then he can whistle, to show you how, and he won't have to laugh."

"The very thing!" cried the parrot. So they tried that way, and they got along quite nicely. Well, by that time it was the dinner hour, and, after the meal, Uncle Wiggily said he would go out again to look for his fortune, and would come back to supper.

"But don't fall into any more molasses cans," cautioned the monkey, and the rabbit gentleman said he would not. Away Uncle Wiggily hopped over the hills, across the fields and through the woods. Pretty soon he came to a pile of nice brown dirt.

"Ha, some one has been digging here," thought the rabbit. "Perhaps some one else is also looking for a fortune of gold or diamonds. If that is so I had better dig here, too."

So, with his sharp paws, the rabbit began to dig in the dirt near the pile of earth. Faster and faster he dug until, all of a sudden, he saw something moving in the hole he had made.

"Ha! I wonder if there is moving-gold here?" he thought.

But when he looked again he saw that it was only a little angle-worm, or earth worm, as some people call them, who was crawling out to sun himself.

"Oh, I hope I haven't hurt you!" exclaimed Uncle Wiggily, kindly, as he lifted up the worm gently in his paws.

"Not a bit of it," answered the worm, twisting about to see if his tail was all there. "But I'm glad you're not a fisherman, Mr. Rabbit."

"Why so?" asked Uncle Wiggily, as he shook some dirt out of his left ear.

"Because if you were you might stick me on a sharp hook and toss me into the water for the fish to eat. Nothing is worse than to have a hook stuck into you," said the worm, moving around until he was in two knots. Then he untied himself again.

"I should think hooks might be unpleasant," spoke the rabbit. "But I won't hurt you, and here is a bit of cherry pie for you."

"Thank you, most kindly," said the angle worm, as he sat up on the end of his tail and ate the cherry pie, juice and all. "But why are you digging in the earth, Uncle Wiggily?"

"To find my fortune," answered the rabbit, and he told how long he had been looking for gold or diamonds and how he hadn't found any yet. "Is there any gold down under the ground where you live?" asked the rabbit, sad-like.

"Not a bit, I'm sorry to say," answered the worm. "I live down there with numbers of my friends, but there is no gold. You had better dig somewhere else. But you have been very kind to me, and if ever I can do you a favor I will."

"Thank you," said Uncle Wiggily, so he hopped out of the hole he had made, and, after saying good-bye to the worm, he traveled on to find another place where he might dig for his fortune.

He came to a place in the woods, where the ground was nice and soft, and there he started to make another hole. Well, he hadn't gone down very far before, all of a sudden, he heard a growling voice behind him calling out:

"Here! Who said you could dig in my land?"

"Oh, I beg your pardon. Is this your land?" asked the rabbit, and he looked up to see the skillery-scalery alligator glaring down at him.

"Yes, this is my land, and these are my woods, and because you were so bold as to dig here I'm going to eat you up!" shouted the 'gator, lashing his double-jointed tail around in the dried leaves. "Here I come!" he cried.

Then he made a dive, with his big, wide-open jaws, down into the hole Uncle Wiggily had dug, but the rabbit didn't wait for him. Out he jumped, and away he hopped, and the 'gator crawled after him. Faster and faster ran the rabbit, and faster and faster came the alligator.

"Oh, I know he'll catch me!" thought poor Uncle Wiggily. "Oh, help! Will no one help me?" he cried.

"Yes, we'll help you!" called a little voice on the ground, and, looking down the rabbit saw the angle worm. And, crawling along with him were about a million other worms, some larger and some smaller than he. "Run along as fast as you can," said the first angle worm, "and we'll twine ourselves in knots around the alligator's legs so that he can't chase you any more. Run! Run!"

"Well, you may be sure Uncle Wiggily ran as hard as he could.

"I'll get you!" cried the alligator, and he made a jump after the rabbit, but it was the last jump the skillery-scalery creature made that day. For the next instant those million angle worms just tied themselves in hard knots, and sailor knots, and bow knots, and double knots, and true lovers' knots and all sorts of knots around the tail and legs of the alligator, and he couldn't move another inch.

"Now's your chance! Hop away, Uncle Wiggily!" cried the first worm. "We'll hold the alligator here because you were so kind to me."

And the rabbit hopped safely away, and the ugly 'gator couldn't even wiggle his double-jointed tail. Then, when the rabbit was safe at the monkey's house, all the angle worms untied their knots off the alligator, and they scurried down into the ground before he could bite them. So that's how it all happened, just as true as I'm telling you. And that 'gator was so angry that he almost bit a piece out of his own tail. Then he went off in the woods and wasn't seen again for some time.

But this wasn't the last of Uncle Wiggily's adventures; no, indeed.

UNCLE WIGGILY'S FORTUNE

The little old lady in the green dress, whose nose and chin nearly touched, was very glad to get the berries which Uncle Wiggily and Kittie Kat gathered. She was very sorry that the wolf had frightened them, but she thought it was just fine of the red monkey to come along when he did.

"And I just wish you could have seen him toss the wolf over the tree-tops by his tail," said the old gentleman rabbit. "It was as good as going to the circus."

"Well, for doing such a trick, the red monkey can have two pieces of my berry pie," spoke the little old woman in the green dress. And that red monkey was very, very thankful, and he ate the two pieces of pie, even down to the last drop of juice.

Of course the rabbit gentleman and Kittie Kat had some pie too, and, after they had eaten their share, and had washed their faces and paws they stayed at the house of the little old woman all night.

"For I want Uncle Wiggily to be nice and rested so he can start off after his fortune tomorrow," she said.

Well, the next morning the rabbit gentleman got ready to go. The old lady with the green dress filled his valise full of good things to eat, including some berry pie, for there were no more cherries now, you know. Then, with Kittie Kat on one side of him and the red monkey on the other side, Uncle Wiggily set off.

"Remember," called the old lady, as she said good-by, "you must travel straight on for three days, and you needn't stop on the way to look for your fortune, for you won't find it. Just keep on, and at the end of the third day you will come to a hill. Go up the hill, and down the other side, and you will then come into your fortune, and I hope you will live for a good many years to enjoy it."

"Thank you so much!" exclaimed the rabbit. "It hardly seems possible that I am going to be rich after all my travels. What kind of a fortune will it be?"

"Oh, you must wait and see," said the kind little old lady.

Well, the rabbit and the pussy girl and the red monkey traveled on and on. The first day they came to a big mountain, and the monkey wanted to climb up it to see if there were any coconut trees growing on the top.

"No," Uncle Wiggily told him. "We must keep straight on the level road until we come to the hill." And it is a good thing they didn't climb that mountain. For on top lived a big giant who had a big club, and he might have hit the red monkey with it. Mind, I'm not saying for sure, but that might have happened, you know.

So the three friends traveled on and on, and at the second day they came to where there was a big ball of blue yarn beside a little lake. It was a nice, soft ball of yarn, such as kittens play with when grandma is knitting warm mittens for winter.

"Oh, I must stop and play with that ball of yarn," said Kittie Kat.

"No," said the rabbit, "you must not do that, for the old lady said we were to keep straight on for three days."

And it is a good thing Kittie Kat didn't roll the ball, for inside of it was a big rat, and he might have bitten the little pussy girl. Mind, I'm not saying for sure, but that might have happened.

"Now, this is the third day," spoke Uncle Wiggily when they got up one morning, after having slept in a hollow stump. "By nightfall we ought to come to the hill, and on the other side will be my fortune. Oh, how glad I am!"

So they kept on and on, stopping for dinner in a nice shady place, and toward evening they came to the hill.

"There it is!" cried the rabbit as he hurried up it. "Oh, I can hardly wait until I get to the other side."

Up he went, and up went the red monkey and up went Kittie Kat. And on the way the bad fuzzy fox sprang out from the bushes and tried to catch them, but Uncle Wiggily tickled him with his crutch and made him sneeze and fall down hill.

Then they came to the top of the hill. The sun was just setting in the clouds, and they were all colored golden and violet and purple, and oh, it was beautiful! Uncle Wiggily came to a stop. On one side was the red monkey and on the other the pussy girl. The rabbit rubbed his eyes. Then he took off his glasses and polished them on his handkerchief. Then he looked down the hill.

"Why—why!" exclaimed Uncle Wiggily. "There must be some mistake. I don't see any gold or diamonds. And this place—why, it's the very place I started away from so many weeks ago! There is where I live—there is where Sammie and Susie Littletail live— that's the tree where Johnnie and Billie Bushytail live, and there is the pond where Alice and Lulu and Jimmie Wibblewobble, the ducks, live! This is home! There can't be a fortune here!"

Oh, how disappointed he felt. The sun sank lower behind the clouds and made them more golden and green and purple.

Then out from their homes ran the rabbit children and the squirrel brothers and the duck children, and Peetie, and Jackie Bow-Wow, and Bully the Frog, and his brother, and Dottie and Munchie Trot, and Buddy and Brighteyes Pigg—and all the others.

"Oh, here is Uncle Wiggily! Our Uncle Wiggily has come back!" they cried, leaping about in joy. "Oh, how glad we are to see you. Happy! Happy welcome! You are rich, Uncle Wiggily! Rich! Very rich!"

"Rich!" said the rabbit, rubbing his eyes and trying to stand up while all his friends gathered around him. "But I don't understand. The little old lady in the green dress said I would find my fortune here, but I don't see it."

"Let me explain," said Sammie Littletail. "Do you see that field of cabbage, Uncle Wiggily?" and the rabbit boy pointed to it.

"Yes," said the rabbit, "I see the field."

"There are seventeen million, two hundred and fifty-six thousand, nine hundred and three cabbages there," said Sammie,

and they are all yours. And do you see that field of turnips?"

"Yes," said Uncle Wiggily, as he looked down the hill, "I see them."

"There are nineteen million, four hundred and thirty-three thousand, eight hundred and sixty-six turnips," said Sammie, "and they are all yours. And do you see that field of carrots?"

"I do," said Uncle Wiggily, but he couldn't see so very far, as tears of joy were in his eyes.

"There are one hundred million, eight hundred and twenty-three thousand nine hundred and ninety-nine and a half carrots in that field," said Sammie. "Jillie Longtail, the mouse, had the half carrot because she was ill, but all the rest are yours, and you are the richest rabbit in the world—the very richest—there is your fortune. You can sell the turnips and carrots and cabbages and have forty-'leven barrels of gold."

"But—but I don't understand," said Uncle Wiggily, as he tried to hug all his friends at once.

"It was this way," said Sammie, "when you were gone we all planted things in your garden and fields for you, and we took care of them, hoeing and watering them, until they grew as never carrots or turnips or cabbages grew before. So now you have come back to us, and you are rich."

And it was true. After traveling almost around the earth in search of his fortune Uncle Wiggily came back to find it right at home, and that's the way it often happens in this world.

Well, you can imagine how surprised he was. He hugged and kissed all his friends and then he went into his old house with Sammie and Susie Littletail, and when he had sold the cabbages and carrots and turnips for many barrels of gold, there he lived for many, many years, as happy an old gentleman rabbit as you could find in a day's journey. And though his rheumatism bothered him at times it couldn't be helped. And he gave all his friends as much money as they wanted, and they all had good times together, and lots of fun, and every once in a while Uncle Wiggily would treat everybody to strawberry ice-cream cones with cabbage or turnip sauce on.

UNCLE WIGGILY AND THE EEL

My, how it did rain! The water just dripped down from the clouds as if it came from a fountain turned wrong side up, and as Uncle Wiggily walked along the seashore beach, with a toadstool held over him for an umbrella he thought he had never seen such a storm.

"But, I can't stay indoors, because it rains," he said to himself as he started out that morning to look for his fortune. "That would never do. A little water can't hurt me, and besides, with this toadstool umbrella, it isn't as bad as it might be."

So he hopped along, leaning on his red-white-and-blue-striped barber-pole crutch, and with his valise strapped to his back, and holding the toadstool umbrella over his head. And he felt so happy in spite of the rain that he sang a little song.

It went something like this, to the tune of "Hum-tum-tum ti tiddle-i-um:"

"I feel so very happy,
　　No matter if it rains,
For I don't ride on trolley cars,
　　Nor yet on railroad trains.

"Whenever I feel thirsty,
　　I take a drink of tea,
Or, if I can't find any,
　　Why, milk will do for me.

"I haven't found my fortune,
　　Perhaps I never can,
But I can hop upon the beach,
　　And beat an old tin pan."

And just then the gentleman rabbit saw an old tin pan lying on the sand, and he went up to it and pounded on it with his crutch. Not hard you understand—not so hard as to hurt it, but enough to make a noise like a drum.

"There, perhaps that will wake the people up," thought the rabbit for the beach was very lonesome in the rainstorm, with no children building sand houses, and no one in bathing. So Uncle Wiggily beat the tin pan again, and made a great racket, and, all of a sudden something glided out from under the pan. It was something long and thin, and it had a long, thin tail.

"Oh, my! It's the bad snake!" cried the rabbit, and he jumped back so quickly that he dropped his toadstool umbrella and the rain came down on the end of his twinkling nose. He was just about to hop away as fast as he could when the long, thin creature, who had been under the tin pan, exclaimed:

"I'm not a snake."

"No? Then pray tell what you are?" asked Uncle Wiggily quickly.

"I am a slippery eel," was the answer. "Just see if you can hold me, and that will show you how slippery I am."

So Uncle Wiggily very politely took hold of the eel by the tail. But, my goodness me, sakes alive and a piece of ice! In an instant that slippery eel had slipped away.

"What did I tell you?" the eel called to the rabbit, as he crawled back toward the tin.

"Well, you are certainly very slippery," said Uncle Wiggily. "I hope I didn't squeeze you too hard."

"Oh, pray do not mention it," said the eel, politely. "I am used to being squeezed, and that's why I'm so slippery; in order that I may get away easily."

"I hope I didn't wake you up from your sleep under the tin pan," went on the rabbit, who was very kind-hearted.

"Pray do not mention that, either," said the slippery eel, who was very polite. "It was time I awakened, anyhow. But, since you have been so nice about it, if ever I can do you a favor please let

me know." Then he stood up on the end of his thin tail and made a low bow, and slipped into the ocean.

"Ha! That is a curious sort of chap," said Uncle Wiggily as he hopped on. "I should like to meet him again, when I have more time to talk to him. But now I must look for my fortune." So he went on looking along the beach in the rain, but never a bit of his fortune could he find.

Now, in a little while, something is going to happen. In fact it's time for it now, so I'll tell you all about it. As Uncle Wiggily was hopping along the beach, where some bushes grew close down to the water, he thought he saw something shining in the sand.

"Perhaps that may be a diamond," he said. "I'll dig it up." So he got a nice pink shell with which to dig, and he set to work, laying aside his toadstool umbrella, and not minding the rain in the least.

Then, all of a sudden, up behind the bushes came sneaking the old fuzzy fox. He had been looking all over for something to eat, but all he could find were hard shell clams, and they were too rough on his teeth, so he couldn't eat them.

"Oh, but there is a soft, delicious morsel!" exclaimed the fox, as he saw Uncle Wiggily digging in the sand, and the fox smacked his lips, and sharpened his teeth on a stone. "Now I will have a good dinner," he added.

So he crept closer and closer to Uncle Wiggily, and the old gentleman rabbit never heard him, for he was busy digging for his fortune.

"Now the thing for me to do," thought the fox, "is to spring out on him before he has a chance to move. And I think I can do it, because his back is toward me, and he can't see."

So the fox got ready to spring right on Uncle Wiggily and maybe carry him off to his den in the woods, and the old gentleman rabbit didn't know a thing about it, but kept on digging for his fortune.

"Here I go!" said the fox to himself, and he crouched down for a spring, just as your kittie does when she plays she is after a mouse. Up into the air leaped the fox, right toward the rabbit. And then, suddenly a voice cried:

"Look out, Uncle Wiggily! Look out!"

The rabbit glanced up, but he was down in the sand hole and he couldn't get out quickly on account of his rheumatism. Right toward him the fox was springing, and then, all at once, the slippery eel—for it was he who had called to the rabbit—the kind eel wiggled up out of the ocean. Up along the beach he crawled quickly, until he was right in front of the rabbit in the hole. Then the eel stretched out like a piece of rope and waited.

And then the fox came down on his four feet, but, instead of landing on Uncle Wiggily he landed right on the slippery eel, and that eel was truly as slippery as a piece of ice. Right out from under him slipped the feet of the old fuzzy fox, and down he fell. Slippery, sloppery, slappery he went, sliding along on the eel until he slid all the way off and plumped into the ocean, where he was nearly drowned, for the water got in his nose and mouth and eyes.

"Now, you can get away, Uncle Wiggily," said the eel, and the rabbit kindly thanked the slippery creature, and grabbed up the shining thing he had dug out of the sand, for he thought it was a diamond. Then the fox slunk away, taking his wet and bushy tail with him, and Uncle Wiggily was safe for that time, anyhow, and the eel wiggled along after the old gentleman rabbit, who thought he had better look for a good place to sleep.

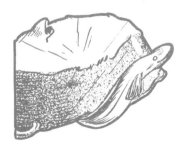

SUSIE AND THE WHITE KITTIE

Susie Littletail had gone for a walk in the woods. It was coming on spring, but the little bunny girl did not go to see if there were any wildflowers peeping up. Indeed, she cared very little about flowers, except the kind that were good to eat, and these were mostly clover blossoms. So that is what Susie went out to look for.

Uncle Wiggily Longears had said to her that day: "It seems to me, Susie, that it's getting quite warm out. My rheumatism is better, and it never does get better unless it's getting warm. So, of course, it must be getting warm."

Susie thought so, too.

"Then if it's getting warmer it must be almost spring," went on her uncle. "Now, if I were you, I would go take a walk and see how the clover is coming on. Some nice, fresh clover would taste very good."

"I'll see if I can get you any," spoke Susie, who was a very good little rabbit girl, and who always was kind to her old uncle. So that is why she was walking in the woods. She was almost through the place where the tall trees grew, and was just going to step out into a field that looked as if it had clover in it, when she heard a funny little noise. It was a sort of a squeak, and at first Susie thought it might be Nurse Jane Fuzzy-Wuzzy, for, sometimes, the muskrat started off with a squeak when she wanted to talk. But it was not her nurse whom Susie saw. Instead it was a dear little pussy kitten.

"Did you make that funny noise?" asked the little rabbit girl of the kitten.

"Yes," answered pussy, "but I don't call it a funny noise."

"I do," went on Susie.

"It was not at all funny, and I don't see anything to laugh at," spoke pussy, and then Susie saw that the white kitten had a large tear in each eye. "That was a mew," the kittie said.

"Why did you mew, pussy?" asked Susie.

"Because I am lost, and I don't know my way home. I guess you would mew if you couldn't find your papa or mamma."

"No," said Susie, "I wouldn't mew, but I would be very much frightened. But why don't you go home?" And Susie sat up and wrinkled her nose, just like water when it bubbles in the tea kettle, for that was the way she smelled, and she wanted to see if she could smell danger.

"How can I go home when I don't know the way?" asked the white kitten.

"Which way did you come in here?"

"If I knew that, I would know which way to go back home," the pussy replied, and the large tears, one in each eye, fell out and dropped on the ground, while two more came into her eyes.

"Are you crying because you are lost?" asked Susie.

"Of course. Wouldn't you?"

"Perhaps," answered Susie. "But you see I never was lost. I can always smell my way home, no matter how far off I go," and she wiggled her nose so fast that it made the kittie quite cross-eyed to watch it, and being cross-eyed made pussy sneeze. Then the pussy felt better.

"Can you show me the way home?" asked the kittie of Susie.

"Not to your house, for I don't know where it is," answered Susie, "but I could show you the way to mine."

Then the white kittie wanted Susie to do this, but the little rabbit girl thought it might not be safe, for the little kittie might show the big cats where the new underground house was.

"What is your name?" asked Susie of the kittie.

"My name is Ann Gora, but every one calls me Ann."

"That is a funny name," said Susie.

"I don't think it is at all," went on the kitten. "It is no funnier than Susie," and she began to cry again.

"Oh, don't cry!" exclaimed Susie, and she patted the kittie on the back with her foot. "Come with me. We will walk through the field, and maybe we will see your house. I think you must live in a house with people, for kitties never live in the woods like the squirrels, or in burrows as we do. We will look until we find a house with people in it, and maybe you belong there."

"That will be fine!" cried the kittie, and she dried her tears on her paw. So Susie and the kittie walked on together. And pretty soon Susie saw a little girl coming toward them. The little girl was looking in the grass, and calling, "Ann—Ann," in a soft voice. And when she saw the little kittie she ran to her and caught her up in her arms and hugged her. Then Susie Littletail ran home, for she was afraid of little girls, and on the way she saw that the clover was coming up nicely, so she told Uncle Wiggily.

HIDING THE EASTER EGGS

What a lot of Easter eggs there were! I'm sure if you tried to count all that Sammie and Susie Littletail, and Papa and Mamma Littletail, to say nothing of Uncle Wiggily Longears and Nurse Jane Fuzzy-Wuzzy had colored, ready for Easter, you never could do it, never, never, never! Of course, Uncle Wiggily couldn't get so very many of the eggs ready for the children, because, you know, he has rheumatism, but then Sammie and Susie were so quick, and Jane Fuzzy-Wuzzy hurried so, that long before Easter Sunday morning, or Easter Monday morning, whenever you children hunt for your eggs, they were all ready.

You see, the rabbits have to hide all the Easter eggs that you children hunt for. Of course, I don't mean those in the store windows; the pretty ones, made of candy, and with little windows that you look through to see beautiful scenes. Oh, no, not those, but the ones you find at home. Those in the windows are put there by different kinds of rabbits.

Well, all the Easter eggs were ready, and Sammie and Susie, their papa and mamma, Uncle Wiggily Longears and Nurse Jane Fuzzy-Wuzzy, set out to hide them. There were many colors. I think I have told you about them, but I'll just mention a few again. There were red ones, blue ones, green ones, pink ones, Alice blue ones, Johnnie red ones, Froggie green ones, strawberry color, and then that new shade, skilligimink, which is very fine indeed, and which turned Sammie sky-blue-pink.

So the rabbits started off with their baskets of colored eggs on their paws.

"Now, be careful, Sammie," called his mamma. "Don't fall

down and break any of those eggs."

"No, mamma," answered Sammie, who was still colored sky-blue-pink, for it hadn't all worn off yet. "I'll be very careful."

"So will I, mamma," called Susie.

So they walked on through the woods to visit Newark and all the places around where children want Easter eggs. Of course, if you had gone out in the woods on top of Orange Mountain you could not have seen those rabbits, because they were invisible. That is, you couldn't see them, because Mrs. Cluck-Cluck, the fairy hen, had given them all cloaks spun out of cobwebs, just like the Emperor of China once had, and this made it so no one could see them. For it would never do, you know, to have the rabbits spied upon when they were hiding the eggs. It wouldn't be fair, any more than it would be right to peek when you're "it" in playing blind man's buff.

Well, pretty soon, after a while, as they all walked through the woods, Sammie kept going slower and slower and slower, because his basket was quite heavy, until he was a long way in back of his papa, his mamma and Susie. But he didn't mind that, for he knew he had plenty of time, when all at once what should come running out of the bushes but a great big dog. At first Sammie was frightened, but then when he looked again he knew the dog was not a rabbit-dog. No, what is worse, he was an egg-dog. Now an egg-dog is a dog that eats eggs, and they are one of the very worst kinds of dogs there are. So the dog saw Sammie and knew what the little rabbit boy had in his basket. But he asked him, making believe he didn't know: "What have you in that basket, my little chap?" You see, he called him "little chap" so as to pretend he was a friendly egg-dog.

"There are Easter eggs in the basket," said Sammie politely.

"And what, pray, are Easter eggs, if I may be so bold as to ask?" inquired the dog, licking his teeth with his long red tongue, and blinking his eyes, as if he didn't care.

"Easter eggs," replied Sammie, "are eggs for children for Easter, and they are very prettily colored."

"Oh, ho!" exclaimed the dog, just like that, and he sniffed the air. "Please excuse me. But would you kindly be so good as to let me see those eggs? I never saw any colored ones."

"Well," answered Sammie, "I am in a hurry, but you may have one peep."

So he opened the top of the basket and there, sure enough, were the eggs, the green, the blue, the pink, the Johnnie red and the skilligimink colored ones and all.

"Oh, how lovely!" cried the bad dog, sniffing the air again. "May I have one?"

"No," said Sammie, very decidedly, "these are for the little children." Then that dog got angry. Oh, you should have seen how angry he got. No, on second thoughts I am glad you did not see how unpleasant he was, for it might spoil your Easter. Anyhow, he was dreadfully angry, dreadfully! He showed his teeth, and he made his hair stand up straight, and he growled: "Give me all those eggs, or I'll take them right away from you! I am an egg-dog, and I must have eggs. Give them to me, I say!"

Well, maybe poor Sammie wasn't frightened! He trembled so that the eggs rattled together and very nearly were broken. Then he started to run away, but the bad dog ran after him, and what do you think? Just as the horrid creature was about to take those lovely Easter eggs out of the basket and eat them up, who should come flying through the woods but Mrs. Cluck-Cluck, the fairy hen! She dashed at that dog, with her feathers sticking out, and made him run off. Then how glad Sammie was! He hurried and caught up to his papa and mamma, and soon all the Easter eggs were hidden.

Oh, what fun Sammie and Susie had running back through the woods after the eggs were all put in the secret places! Susie found a turnip in a field, and Sammie a carrot, and they ate them as they hopped along. Uncle Wiggily walked quite slowly, for his rheumatism was bothering him, and when those rabbits got home to the burrow, what do you think they found? Why, there were invitations for them all to come to a party that was going to be given by Lulu and Alice Wibblewobble. Alice and Lulu were little duck girls, and they lived with their papa and mamma, Mr. and Mrs. Wibblewobble, in a pen, not far from the rabbit burrow. They had a brother named Jimmie, but it wasn't his birthday, for he was a day older than his sisters, who were twins. That is their birthdays came at the same time. Some day I'm going to tell you a lot of stories about these same ducks.

"May we go to the party, mamma?" asked Susie.

"Of course," answered Mamma Littletail, and they all went, even Nurse Jane Fuzzy-Wuzzy. They had a fine time, which I will tell you about in another book that has a lot of duck stories in it. But I just want to mention one thing that occurred.

Just as the party was over, and every one was coming home, Uncle Wiggily couldn't find his crutch, which Nurse Jane Fuzzy-Wuzzy had gnawed out of a cornstalk for him. Finally he did find it behind the door. Then he, and Sammie and Susie, and Mr. and Mrs. Littletail started for the burrow.

Then, all at once, when they were in the front yard of the Wibblewobble home, if a silver trumpet didn't sound in the woods: "Ta-ra-ta-ra-ta-ra!" just like that, and up came riding a little boy, all in silver and gold, on a white horse. He wanted to know if he was too late for the party, the little boy did, and when Uncle Wiggily said yes, the little boy was much disappointed.

Then Uncle Wiggily asked him who he was, and the little boy said:

"I am the fairy prince! I used to be a mud turtle, and live in the pond where Lulu and Alice and Jimmie Wibblewobble swim. But I got tired of being a mud turtle, though I *was* a fairy prince, so I changed myself into a little boy."

But, do you know, Uncle Wiggily didn't believe him, and, what's more, he said so. Oh, yes, indeed he did! Then what did that little boy-fairy-prince do, but up and say:

"Well, you soon will believe me, Uncle Wiggily. You come back to the woods a little later, and something wonderful will happen. I'll make you believe in fairies; that's what I will, for you will see a red fairy very shortly."

But still Uncle Wiggily didn't believe, and he went home, moving his nose and ears at the same time.

SUSIE AND THE BLUE FAIRY

They were talking about Uncle Wiggily's visit to the red fairy, in the rabbits' burrow the next day, when Susie remarked:

"Well, if I saw a fairy, I think I'd ask for something more magical than having my rheumatism cured."

"No you wouldn't," said her uncle, as he nibbled a bit of chocolate-covered carrot that Nurse Jane Fuzzy-Wuzzy had made. "You think you would, but you wouldn't. In the first place, you never had rheumatism, or you'd be glad to get the first fairy you saw to cure it. And in the second place, when you see a fairy it makes you feel so funny you don't know what you are saying. But I am certainly glad I met that one. I never felt better in all my life than I do since my rheumatism is cured. I believe I'll dance a jig."

"Oh, no, don't," begged Mamma Littletail.

"Yes, I shall too," spoke Uncle Wiggily. "Begging your pardon, of course, Alvinah." You see, Mamma Littletail's first name was Alvinah. So Uncle Wiggily danced a jig, and did it fairly well, considering everything.

That afternoon Susie Littletail went for a walk in the woods. She was all alone, for Sammie had gone over to play with Bully, the frog, and Billie and Johnnie Bushytail, his squirrel chums. Susie walked along, and she was rather hoping she might meet the fairy prince, who was changed from a mud turtle into a nice boy, and came to Lulu and Alice Wibblewobble's party. But Susie didn't meet him, and, when it began to get dark, she started for home.

"Oh!" she exclaimed aloud, as she came to a little spot where the grass grew nice and green, and where the trees were all set in a circle, just as if they were playing, Ring Around the Rosy, Sweet Tobacco Posey. "Oh, dear, I wish I would meet with a fairy, as Uncle Wiggily did! But I don't s'pose I ever will. I never have any good luck! Only last week I lost my ring with the blue stone in it."

And just then—oh, in fact, right after Susie finished speaking, what should she hear but a voice singing. Yes, a voice singing; a sweet, silvery voice, and this is what it sang. Of course, I can't sing this in a sweet, silvery voice, but I'll do the best I can. Now this is the song:

"If any one is seeking
 A fairy for to see,
If they will kindly glance up
 Into this chestnut tree
They'll see what they are seeking,
 I'm truly telling you,
For I'm a little fairy
 All dressed in baby-blue."

Then, you may believe me or not, if Susie didn't look up into the tree, and there, in a hole where the Owl school teacher once lived, was a really and truly-ruly fairy. Honest. Susie knew at once it was a fairy that she saw because the little creature was colored baby blue, you know, the shade they put on babies, and she had gauzy wings, with stars on them, and carried a magic wand which also had a star on it, did the little blue creature. Still, the little rabbit girl wanted to make sure, so she asked: "Are you a fairy?"

"I am," replied the little creature in blue. "Can you kindly tell me how much two and two are?"

"Four," answered Susie.

"Is it really?"

"Of course. You ought to know that," spoke Susie proudly, for she was at the head of her arithmetic class.

"Ought I?" asked the fairy with a sigh. "Well, I suppose I had, but I haven't been to school in ever so long—not since I was a wee bit of a child, and that's ever and ever so many years ago, when I was no bigger than that," and she pointed to something in the air.

"Bigger than what?" asked Susie, who didn't see anything.

"Than that speck of star dust," went on the blue fairy. "It's so small you can't see it. But no matter. Because you were so kind as to tell me how much two and two are, I will give you three wishes."

"Will you, really?" cried Susie in delight.

"Yes, three wishes, for I am a regular fairy, and that is the regular number of wishes you may have. Some fairies only give two wishes, and some only one. But I always give three. Go ahead now, and wish."

"Let me see," thought Susie, and her nose twinkled like three stars, she was so excited. "First I wish for a golden coach drawn by four horses."

"Oh!" cried the fairy, "I'm so sorry, for wishes like that, though they come true, never last. Still, you may have it," and she waved her magic wand, and if the golden coach and four horses didn't appear right there in the woods—honest! "Wish again, my dear," went on the fairy, and this time Susie was more careful.

"I wish for ten boxes of chocolate-covered carrots," she said, and once more the fairy said she was sorry, for that wish wouldn't last. Still, it came true, and down from the tree where the blue fairy sat, came tumbling the ten boxes of chocolate-covered carrots, each one wrapped up in lace paper. Susie put them in the golden coach, and was ready for her next wish. She thought a good long while over this one. Then she said:

"I wish I could find my ring with the blue stone!"

At that the fairy clapped her tiny hands. "That is a fine wish!" she cried. "It will come true, and stay so. But the others——" and she shook her head sorrowfully. Then she waved her magic wand three times in the air, and suddenly, in less than two jumps, if the ring with the blue stone, that Susie had lost, didn't appear right on the end of the wand. And it flew off and landed right on Susie's paw. Oh, wasn't she glad! And the fairy said: "The ring will last, because that is blue, and I am blue, too. Now, good-by, Susie." And with that she disappeared, changing into a butterfly with golden wings. Then Susie started to get in the golden coach and ride home, but, would you believe me, if those horses didn't run away, upsetting the coach and breaking it, and scattering all the ten boxes of chocolate-covered carrots all over. Oh, how badly Susie felt, but it was just what the fairy said would happen. The first two wishes didn't last. Anyhow, Susie had the ring, and she hurried home to tell her story.

SAMMIE AND THE GREEN FAIRY

When Susie told her brother Sammie about what happened to her in the woods, when she saw the blue fairy, the little rabbit boy remarked:

"Aw, I guess you fell asleep and dreamed that, Susie." for that's the way with brothers sometimes. I once had a brother, and he——but there, I'll tell you about him some other time.

"No," answered Susie, "I didn't dream it. Why, here's my ring to prove it," and she held out the one with the blue stone in it.

"I guess you found that in the woods, where you lost it," went on Sammie. "I don't believe in fairies at all."

"But didn't one cure Uncle Wiggily's rheumatism?"

"Aw, well, I guess that would have gotten better anyhow."

"It wouldn't, so there!" exclaimed Susie. "I just hope you see a fairy some day, and I hope they don't treat you as kind as the one treated me, even if the horses did run away and disappear." But of course Susie didn't really want anything bad to happen to her brother. But you just wait and see what did happen. Oh, it was something very, very strange, yes, indeed, and I'm not fooling a bit; no, indeed. I wouldn't make it out anything different than what it really was, not for a penny and a half.

Well, it happened about a week later. Sammie was coming home from a ball game, which he had played with Johnnie and Billie Bushytail (of whom I will tell you later), and some others of his chums, and he was in a deep, dark part of the wood, when suddenly he heard a crashing in the bushes.

"Pooh!" exclaimed Sammie. "I s'pose that's one of them fairies. I'm not going to notice her," and with that he tossed his baseball up in the air, careless like, to show that he didn't mind. But he was a bit nervous, all the same, and his hand slipped and his best ball went right down in a deep, dark, muddy puddle of water. Then Sammie felt pretty bad, I tell you, and he was going to get a stick to fish the ball out, when he heard the crashing in the bushes again, and what should appear but—no, not a fairy, but a bad, ugly fox.

"Ah!" exclaimed the fox, looking at Sammie, and smacking his lips, "I've been waiting for you for some time."

"Yes?" asked the little boy rabbit, and he tried to see a way to run past that fox, only there wasn't any.

"Yes, really," went on the fox. "Have you had your supper?"

"No," replied Sammie, "I haven't."

"Neither have I," continued the fox, "but I'm going to have it pretty soon, in fact, almost immediately," which you children know means right away. "I'm going to eat directly," went on that bad fox, and he smacked his lips again and looked at Sammie, as if he was going to eat him up, for that's really what he meant when he said he was going to have supper. Oh, how frightened Sammie was. He began to tremble, and he wished he'd started for home earlier. Then the fox crouched down and was just going to jump on that little boy rabbit, when something happened.

Right up from that puddle of water, where Sammie had lost his ball, sprang a little man in green. He was green all over, like Bully, the frog, but the funny part of it was that he wasn't wet a bit, even though he came up out of the water.

"Ha! What have we here?" he cried out, just like that.

"If—if you please, sir," began Sammie.

"It's my supper time!" cried the fox, interrupting, which was not very polite on his part. "It's my supper time, and I'm hungry."

"I don't see anything to eat," spoke the little green man. "Nothing at all," and he looked all around.

"If—if you please, kind sir," went on Sammie, "I think he intends to eat me."

"What! What!" cried the little green man. "The very idea! The very idonical idea! We'll see about that! Oh, my, yes, and a bushel of apple turnovers besides! Aha! Ahem!"

Then he looked most severely at that fox, most severely, I do assure you, and he asked: "Were you going to eat up my friend Sammie Littletail?"

"I was, but I didn't know he was a friend of yours," replied the fox, beginning to tremble. Oh, you could see right away that he was afraid of that little green man.

"Oh, you bad fox, you!" cried the little green man. "Oh, you bad fox! Just for that I'm going to turn you into a little country village! Presto, chango! Smacko, Mackeo! Bur-r-r-r!" and he waved his hands at the fox, who immediately disappeared. And he was changed into a little country village, with a church, a school and thirty-one houses, and it's called Foxtown to this very day. I ought to know, for I used to live there.

"Well, Sammie?" asked the little green man, when the fox had vanished, "How do you feel now?"

"Much better, kind sir. Thank you. But who are you?"

"Me? Who am I? Why, don't you know?"

"No, indeed, unless you're some relation to Bully, the frog."

"Well, I am a sort of distant thirty-second cousin to him. I am the green fairy. And to prove it, look here, I will get your ball back for you."

Then while Sammie looked on, his eyes getting bigger and bigger and his breath coming faster and faster, until it was like a locomotive or a choo-choo, whatever you call them, going up hill, if that little green man didn't wave his hands over that puddle of water, where Sammie's ball had fallen. And he spoke the magic word, which must never be spoken except on Friday nights, so if you read this on any night but Friday you must skip it, and wait. The word is (Tirratarratorratarratirratarratum), and I put it in brackets, so there would be no mistake. Well, all of a sudden, after the magic word was spoken, if Sammie's ball didn't come bounding up out of that water, and it was as dry as a bone, and it had a nice, new, clean, white cover on.

"There," said the little green man proudly, "I guess that's doing some tricks in the fairy line, isn't it?"

"It certainly is," agreed Sammie, "I can't thank you enough."

"Just believe in fairies after this," said the little green man, as he changed into a bumble bee and flew off.

SUSIE AND THE FAIRY GODMOTHER

You can just imagine how excited Susie and her mamma and papa and Nurse Jane Fuzzy-Wuzzy, the muskrat, were when Sammie got home and told about the bad fox who had been changed into a country village. Uncle Wiggily Longears was surprised, too. He said:

"My, it does seem to me that there are strange goings on in these woods. There never used to be any fairies here. I wonder where they come from?"

"Well, it's a good thing that fox has been changed into a town," spoke Papa Littletail. "If he hadn't been, I would have had him arrested for frightening you, Sammie. I know the policeman down at our corner, and I'm sure he would have arrested him for me. But it's all right now," and Sammie's papa sat back in his chair and read the paper, for he was tired that night from working in the turnip factory. You see, he changed from the carrot factory, and got a place sorting turnips. And sometimes he would bring little sweet ones home to the children.

One day Susie was hurrying back from the store with a loaf of bread, a yeast cake and three-and-a-half of granulated sugar, and she was sort of wondering if she would meet the blue fairy again when, just as she got opposite a place where some goldenrod grew, she heard a voice saying:

"Oh, dear! Oh, dear me! I shall never be able to reach it! Never, never, never!" Susie looked around, and what should she see but a nice, little old lady, trying to break off a stem of goldenrod.

"Oh, dear me suz-dud!" cried the old lady again, and then Susie saw that she was very little indeed, hardly larger than a ten-cent plate of ice cream after it's all melted. So she couldn't reach the goldenrod, she was so little.

"What is the matter?" asked Susie very politely. "Can I help you?"

"Thank you, my dear child," went on the little old lady. "If you would be so kind as to reach me down a stem of goldenrod, I would be very much obliged to you."

"What do you want with it?" asked Susie, wondering who the little old lady could possibly be.

"Why, I want it for a fairy wand," she answered. "I have lost mine."

"Are you a fairy, too?" asked the little rabbit girl, and she began to wonder what would happen next as she broke off a stem for the old lady.

"Indeed I am," replied the little old lady. "I am a fairy god-mother. I have charge of all the other fairies, the blue fairy and the red fairy and the green fairy, and all the other colors, including the fairy prince, who used to be a mud turtle."

"But, if you are a fairy," asked Susie, "why couldn't you make that goldenrod come down to you, when you weren't tall enough to reach up to it?"

"Hush!" exclaimed the fairy godmother, for she really was one, as you shall see. "Hush, my dear child! It's a great secret. Don't tell any one," and she put her right hand over her mouth and her left hand over her ear, and held the goldenrod under her arm. "You see, I lost my magic wand," she went on, "and I couldn't do any more magic until I got a new one. Now I am all right, and to reward you you may come with me."

"But I have to get home with the bread and sugar and yeast cake," said Susie.

"No," spoke the fairy godmother, "you will not need to be in a hurry. Besides, what I will show you will happen in an instant, and you will get home in time after all."

So she waved the goldenrod in the air, and once more the silver trumpet sounded: "Ta-ra-ta-ra-ta-ra!" and, all of a sudden, Susie found herself lifted up, and there she and the fairy god-mother were sailing right through the air on a big burdock leaf. At first Susie was afraid, but she soon got over her fright and

enjoyed the ride.

"Where are we going?" she asked.

"We are going to where the fairies live," answered the little old woman, but she seemed larger now, and the old dress she had worn had changed into a cloak of gold and silver with diamonds and rubies on it all over, like frost on a cold morning.

So pretty soon—oh, I guess in about as long as it would take to eat a peanut, or, maybe, two, if they didn't come to fairyland. At least that's what Susie thought it was, for there were fairies all about. The red fairy was there, and the green, and the blue one. And the blue fairy asked: "Have you your ring yet, Susie?" Then Susie said she had, but she didn't want to talk any more, for so many wonderful things were going on.

The fairies were skipping about, leaping here and there, some riding on the backs of birds and butterflies and bumblebees, and some running in and out of holes in the ground.

"What are they doing?" asked Susie, moving her long ears back and forth.

"They are doing kind things to the people of the earth," replied the fairy godmother, "and it keeps them busy, let me tell you." Then Susie saw fairies doing all sorts of magical tricks, such as making lemonade out of lemons, and things like that.

Then, all at once, just when one little fairy was making a hat out of some straw, the godmother said: "It is time for us to go now," so the burdock leaf came sailing through the air, and Susie got on. As they came near the woods where the goldenrod grew they saw a boy throwing a stone at a robin.

"Ah, I must stop that!" cried the fairy godmother, so she waved her new magic wand that Susie had helped her get, and, honestly, if that stone didn't turn right around in the air, and instead of hitting the bird, it flew back and hit that boy right on the end of his nose! Oh, how he cried, and, what is better, he never threw stones at birds again. I call that a pretty good trick, don't you? Well, the burdock leaf came to the ground, and Susie ran home, and she was just in time to help her mother set bread.

SUSIE AND THE FAIRY CARROT

Susie and Sammie Littletail had been off in the woods for a walk, and to gather some flowers, for they expected company at the underground house, and they wanted it to look nice. Mr. and Mrs. Bushytail and Billie and Johnnie and Sister Sallie were coming, and Susie and her brother hoped to have a very nice time.

Well, they wandered on, and on, and on, and had gathered quite a number of flowers, when Sammie said:

"Come on, we've got enough; let's go home."

"No," answered Susie, "I want to get some sky-blue-pink ones. I think they are so pretty."

"I don't," answered her brother, for that color always reminded him of the time he fell in the dye pot, when they were coloring Easter eggs. "I'm going home. Yellow, and red, and blue, and white flowers are good enough. I don't want any fancy colors."

"Well, you go home and I'll come pretty soon," said his sister, so while Sammie turned back, the little rabbit girl kept on. Oh, I don't know how far she went, but it was a good distance, I'm sure, but still she couldn't seem to find that sky-blue-pink flower. She looked everywhere for it, high and low, and even sideways, which is a very good place; but she couldn't find it. And she kept on going, hoping every minute it would happen to be behind a stump or under a bush. But no, it wasn't.

And then, all of a sudden, about as quick as you can shut your eyes and open them again, if Susie wasn't lost! Yes, sir, lost in those woods all alone. She looked all around, and she didn't know where she was. She'd never been so far away from home before, and, oh, how frightened she was! But she was a brave little rabbit girl, and she didn't cry, that is, at first. No, she started to try to find her way back, but the more she tried the more lost she became, until she was all turned around, you know, like when they blindfold you and turn you around three times before they let you try to pin the tail on the cloth donkey at a party. Yes, that's how it was.

Well, then Susie began to cry, and I don't blame her a bit. I think I would do the same myself. Yes, she sat right down and cried. Then she felt hungry and she looked around for something to eat, and what should she see, right there in the woods, but a carrot.

"Oh!" she cried, "how lucky! Now I shan't be hungry, anyhow." So she picked up the carrot and started to eat it, when all at once that carrot spoke to her. What's that? You don't see how a carrot could speak? Well, it did all the same. But you just listen, please, and maybe you'll see how it happened.

"Please don't eat me," the carrot said, in a squeaky voice.

"Why not?" asked Susie, who was very much surprised.

"Because I am a fairy carrot," it went on. Now do you see how it could speak? Well, I guess! "Yes, I am a fairy carrot, Susie, and I can help you. What do you want most?" it asked.

"I want to find my way home," said the little rabbit girl.

"Very well, my dear," went on the vegetable. "Place me on the ground in front of you, stand on your hind legs, wiggle your left ear, and see what happens."

So Susie did this, and would you believe me, for I'm not exaggerating the least bit, if that fairy carrot didn't roll right along on the ground in front of Susie.

"Follow, follow, follow me,
And you soon at home will be,"

the carrot said, in a sing-song voice, and it rolled on, still more, and Susie followed.

First the carrot went through a deep, dark part of the woods, but Susie wasn't at all afraid, for she believed in fairies. Then, pretty soon, the carrot came to a great big hole. It was too big to jump over, and too deep to crawl down into, and too wide to run around.

"Oh, dear!" cried Susie, "I don't see how I'm going to get over this." But do you s'pose that carrot was bothered? No, sir; not the least bit. It stretched out, like a piece of rubber, and stuck itself across that hole until it was a regular little bridge, and Susie could walk safely over. Then it became an ordinary fairy carrot again, and rolled on in front of her, showing her just which way to go.

After a while she came to a great big lake, one she had never seen before.

"Oh, how shall we get over this?" cried Susie.

"Don't worry," spoke the carrot. Then what did it do but turn into a little boat, and Susie got into it, and sailed over that lake as nicely as you please. Then it turned into an ordinary, garden, fairy carrot again, and rolled on, Susie following. Pretty soon they came to a place where the woods and brush were all on fire.

"Oh, I know we shall never get over that place!" exclaimed Susie, for she was very much afraid of fire, because she once burned a hole in her apron.

"Oh, we'll get over that," promised the carrot. "Just you watch me!" And really truly, if it didn't turn into a rainstorm, and sprinkle down on the flames, and put that fire out, and then, just so Susie wouldn't get wet it turned into an umbrella; and held itself over her all the rest of the way home. So Susie got safely back to the burrow, with all the flowers but the sky-blue-pink one, and maybe she wasn't glad! And maybe her folks weren't glad too! They had begun to worry about her, and Sammie was just going to start off to look for her. So Susie told how the fairy carrot had brought her home, and Uncle Wiggily said:

"Well, there are certainly queer things happening nowadays. I never would have believed it if you hadn't told me."

UNCLE WIGGILY AND THE SKY-CRACKER

Let me see, I think I promised to tell you a story about Uncle Wiggily and the skyrocket, didn't I? Or was it to be about a firecracker, seeing that it soon may be the Fourth of July? What's that—a firecracker—no? A skyrocket? Oh, I'm all puzzled up about it, so I guess I'll make it a sky-cracker, a sort of half-firecracker and half-skyrocket, and that will do.

Well, after Uncle Wiggily had gotten a little yellow bird, that looked like gold, out from the string-trap in a tree, the old gentleman rabbit spent two nights visiting a second cousin of Grandfather Prickly Porcupine, who lived in the woods. Then Uncle Wiggily got up one morning, dressed himself very carefully, combed out his whiskers, and said:

"Well, I'm off again to seek my fortune."

"It's too bad you can't seem able to find it," said the second cousin to Grandfather Prickly Porcupine, "but perhaps you will have good luck to-day. Only you want to be very careful."

"Why?" asked the old gentleman rabbit.

"Well, because you know it will soon be the Fourth of July, and some boys may tie a firecracker or a skyrocket to your tail," said the porcupine.

"Ha! Ha!" laughed Uncle Wiggily. "They will have a hard time doing that, for my tail is so short that the boys would burn their fingers if they tried to tie a firecracker to it."

"Then look out that they don't fasten a skyrocket to your long ears," said the second cousin to Grandfather Prickly Porcupine, as he wrapped up some lettuce and carrot sandwiches for Uncle

Wiggily to take with him.

The old gentleman rabbit said he would watch out, and away he started, going up hill and down hill with his barber-pole crutch as easily as if he was being wheeled in a baby carriage.

"Well, I don't seem to find any fortune," he said to himself as he walked along, and, just as he said that he saw something sparkling in the grass beside the path in the woods. "What's that?" he cried. "Perhaps it is a diamond. If it is I can sell it and get rich." Then he happened to think what the second cousin of Grandfather Prickly Porcupine had told him about Fourth of July coming, and Uncle Wiggily said:

"Ha! I had better be careful. Perhaps that sparkling thing is a spark on a firecracker. Ah, ha!"

So he looked more carefully, and the bright object sparkled more and more, and it didn't seem to be fire, so the old gentleman rabbit went up close, and what do you suppose it was?

Why, it was a great big dewdrop, right in the middle of a pur-ple violet, that was growing underneath a shady fern. Oh, how beautiful it was in the sunlight, and Uncle Wiggily was glad he had looked at it. And pretty soon, as he was still looking, a big, buzzing bumble bee buzzed along and stopped to take a sip of the dewdrop.

"Ha! That is a regular violet ice cream soda for me!" said the bee to Uncle Wiggily. And just as he was taking another drink a big, ugly snake made a spring and tried to eat the bee, but Uncle Wiggily hit the snake with his crutch and the snake crawled away very much surprised.

"Thank you very much," said the bee to the rabbit. "You saved my life, and if ever I can do you a favor I will," and with that he buzzed away.

Well, pretty soon, not so very long, in a little while, Uncle Wiggily came to a place in the woods where there were a whole lot of packages done up in paper lying on the ground. And there was a tent near them, and it looked as if people lived in the white tent, only no one was there just then.

"I guess I'd better keep away," thought the old gentleman rabbit, "or they may catch me." And just then he saw something like a long, straight stick, standing up against a tree. "Ha, that will be a good stick to take along to chase the bears away with," he thought. "I think no one wants it, so I'll take it."

Well, he walked up and took hold of it in his paws, but, mind you, he didn't notice that on one end of the stick was a piece of powder string, like the string of a firecracker, sticking down, and this string was burning. No, the poor old gentleman rabbit never noticed that at all. He started to take the stick away with him when, all of a sudden, something dreadful happened.

With a whizz and a rush and a roar that stick shot into the air, carrying Uncle Wiggily with it, just like a balloon, for he hadn't time to let go of it.

Up and up he went, with a roar and a swoop, and just then he saw a whole lot of boys rushing out of the woods toward the white tent. And one boy cried:

"Oh, fellows, look! A rabbit has hold of our sky-cracker and it's on fire and has gone off and taken him with it! Oh the poor rabbit! Because when the sky-cracker gets high enough in the air the firecracker part of it will go off with a bang, and he'll be killed. Oh, how sorry I am. The hot sun must have set fire to the powder string."

You see those boys had come out in the woods to have their Fourth of July, where the noise wouldn't make any one's head ache.

Well, Uncle Wiggily went on, up and up, with the sky-cracker, and he felt very much afraid for he had heard what the boys said.

"Oh, this is the end of me!" he cried, as he held fast to the sky-cracker. "I'll never live to find my fortune now. When this thing explodes, I'll be dashed to the ground and killed."

The sky-cracker was whizzing and roaring, and black smoke was pouring out of one end, and Uncle Wiggily thought of all his friends whom he feared he would never see again, when all of a sudden along came flying the buzzing bumble bee, high in the air.

He was much surprised to see Uncle Wiggily skimming along on the tail of a sky-cracker.

"Oh, can't you save me?" cried the rabbit.

"Indeed I will, if I can," said the bee, "because you were so kind to me. You are too heavy, or I would fly down to earth with you myself, but I'll do the next best thing. I'll fly off and get Dickie and Nellie Chip-Chip, the sparrow children, and they'll come with a big basket and catch you so you won't fall."

No sooner said than done. Off flew the bee. Quickly he found Dickie and Nellie and told them the danger Uncle Wiggily was in.

"Quick," called Dickie to Nellie. "We must save him."

Off they flew like the wind, carrying a grocery basket between them. Right under Uncle Wiggily they flew, and just as the sky-cracker was going to burst with a "slam-bang!" the old gentleman rabbit let go, and into the basket he safely fell and the sparrow children flew to earth with him. Then the sky-cracker burst all to pieces for Fourth of July, but Uncle Wiggily wasn't on it to be hurt, I'm glad to say.

He spent the Fourth visiting the bumble bee's family, and had ice cream and cake and lemonade for supper, and at night he heard the band play, and he gave Nellie and Dickie ten cents for ice-cream sodas, and that's all to this story.

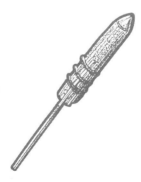

UNCLE WIGGILY AND JACK-IN-THE-PULPIT

Uncle Wiggily was slowly hopping along through the woods, sometimes leaning on his crutch, when his rheumatism pained him, and again skipping along when he got out into the warm sunshine. It was the day after a picnic, and the old gentleman rabbit felt a bit lonesome as all his friends had gone back to their homes.

"I do declare!" exclaimed Uncle Wiggily, as he walked slowly along by a little lake, where an August rabbit was running his motor boat, "if I don't find my fortune pretty soon I won't have any vacation this year. I must look carefully to-day, and see if I can't find a pot full of gold."

Well, he looked as carefully as he could, but my land sakes and a pair of white gloves! he couldn't seem to find a smitch of gold and not so much as a crumb of diamonds.

"Hum!" exclaimed Uncle Wiggily, "at this rate I guess I'll have to keep on traveling for several years before I find my fortune. But never mind, I'm having a good time, anyhow. I'll keep on searching."

So he kept on, and all of a sudden when he was walking past a prickly briar bush, he heard a voice calling:

"Hey, Uncle Wiggily, come on in here."

"Ha! Who are you, and why do you want me to come in there?" asked the old gentleman rabbit.

"Oh, I am a friend of yours," was the answer, "and I will give you a lot of money if you come in here."

"Let me see your face," asked the rabbit, "I want to know who you are."

"Oh! I have a dreadful toothache," said the creature hiding in the bushes. "I don't want to stick my face out in the cold. But if you will take my word for it I am a good friend of yours. I would like very much for you to come in here."

"Well, perhaps I had better," said the old gentleman rabbit, "for I certainly need money."

And he was just going to crawl in under the prickly briar bush when all of a sudden he happened to look, and he saw the skillery-scallery tail of the alligator accidentally sticking out. Yes, it was the alligator trying to fool dear old Uncle Wiggily.

"Oh, ho!" cried the wise old rabbit. "I guess I won't go in there after all," so he hopped to one side and the alligator kept waiting for him to come in so he could eat him, but when the rabbit didn't come in the savage creature with the skillery-scalery tail cried:

"Well, aren't you coming in?"

"No, thank you," said the rabbit. "I have to go on to seek my fortune," and away he hopped. Well, that alligator was so angry that he gnashed his teeth and nearly broke them, and he crawled after Uncle Wiggily, but of course, he couldn't catch him.

Uncle Wiggily was pretty careful after that, and whenever he came near a prickly briar bush he listened with both his long ears stuck up straight to see if he could hear any sounds like an alligator. But he didn't, and so he kept on.

Well, it was coming on toward evening, one afternoon, and the old gentleman rabbit was tramping along the road, wondering where he would sleep, when all of a sudden something came bursting out of the bushes toward the rabbit, and a voice cried out:

"Hide! Hide! Uncle Wiggily. Hide as quickly as you can!"

"Why should I hide?" asked the old gentleman rabbit. "Is there a giant coming after me?"

"Worse than a giant," said the voice. "It is a bad wolf that jumped out of his cage from the circus, and he is just ready to eat up anything he sees," and the July bug, for it was he who had

fluttered out of the bushes, to tell Uncle Wiggily, made his wings go slowly to and fro like an electric palm-leaf fan.

"A wolf, eh?" cried the old gentleman rabbit. "And do you think he will eat me?"

"He surely will," said the July bug. "I happened to fly past his house, and I heard him say to his wife that he was going out to see if he could find a rabbit supper. So I know he's coming for you. You'd better hide."

"Oh! where can I hide?" asked the rabbit, as he looked around for a hollow stump. But there wasn't any, and there were no holes in the ground, and he didn't know what to do.

Then, all at once there was a crashing in the bushes and it sounded like an elephant coming through, breaking all the sticks in his path.

"There's the wolf! There's the wolf!" cried the July bug. "Hide, Uncle Wiggily," and then the bug perched on the high limb of a tree where the wolf couldn't catch him.

Well, the poor old gentleman rabbit looked for a place to hide himself away from the wolf but he couldn't seem to find any, and he was just going to crawl under a stone and maybe hurt himself, when all at once he heard a voice say:

"Jump up here, Uncle Wiggily. I'll hide you from the wolf."

So the rabbit traveler looked up, and there he saw a flower called Jack-in-the-pulpit looking down on him. When you pick a wood-bouquet you put them in with some ferns to make the bouquet look pretty. They are a flower like a vase, with a top curling over, and a thing standing up in the centre whose name is "Jack."

"Jump in here," said the Jack. "I'll fold my top down over you like an umbrella, and the wolf can't find you."

"But you are so small that I can't get inside," said the rabbit.

"Oh, I'll make myself bigger," cried the Jack, and he took a long breath, and puffed himself up and swelled himself up, until he was large enough for Uncle Wiggily to jump down inside. Then the Jack-in-the-pulpit closed down the umbrella top over the rabbit, and he was hidden away as nice and snug as could be wished.

Pretty soon that bad savage wolf came prancing along, and he looked all over for the rabbit. Then he sniffed and cried:

"Ha! I smell him somewhere around here! I'll find him!" But he couldn't see Uncle Wiggily because he was safely hidden in the Jack-in-the-pulpit. So the wolf raged around some more and chased after his tail, and just as he smelled the rabbit hidden in the flower, the July bug flew down out of the tree, bang! right into the eyes of the wolf, and then the savage creature felt so badly that he ran home and ate cold bread and water for supper, and he didn't bother Uncle Wiggily any more that day.

So that's how the Jack-in-the-pulpit saved the rabbit and very thankful Uncle Wiggily was. And he stayed that night in a hollow stump, and the next day he went on to seek his fortune.

UNCLE WIGGILY AND THE PEANUT MAN

After Uncle Wiggily and an elephant and a big dog had eaten up some ice cream cones, they sat in the woods a while and looked at the place where the watery lake had been before the elephant drank it up to save a rabbit from drowning.

"My, but you must be strong to take up all that water," said the dog.

"Yes, I guess I am pretty strong," said the elephant, though he was not at all proud-like. "I will show you how I can pull up a tree," he said. So he wound his trunk around a big tree and he gave one great, heaving pull and up that tree came by the roots. Then, all of a sudden a voice cried:

"Oh, you're upsetting all my eggs!" and a robin, who had her nest in the tree, fluttered around feeling very sad.

"Oh, excuse me, Mrs. Robin," said the elephant. "I would not have disturbed you for the world had I known that your nest was in that tree. I'll plant it right back again in the same place I pulled it up. Anyhow, I intended to do it, as it is not a good thing to kill a tree. I'll plant it again."

So he put the tree back in the hole, and with his big feet he stamped down the earth around it. Then the robin's nest and eggs were safe, and she sang a pretty song because she was thankful to the elephant.

Well, the elephant had to sleep out-of-doors again that night, because he couldn't find a house large enough for him, but Uncle Wiggily slept in the big dog's kennel. In the morning the rabbit said:

"It is very nice here, and I like it very much, but I must travel along, I s'pose, and see if I can't find my fortune. Are you coming, Mr. Elephant?"

"Why, certainly. I will go along with you," said the big chap. "Perhaps the dog will come also."

"No, thank you," said the dog. "I am going to meet a friend of mine, named Percival, and we are going to call on Lulu and Alice and Jimmie Wibblewobble, the duck children."

"Is that so?" exclaimed Uncle Wiggily. "Why, Percival and the Wibblewobbles are friends of mine. Kindly give them my love and say that I hope soon to get back home with my fortune."

So the dog said he would, and he started off to meet Percival, who used to work in the same circus where the elephant came from. And the rabbit and the elephant hurried off together down the road.

"Are you ever going back to the circus?" asked Uncle Wiggily of the elephant as they went along.

"Not unless they catch me and make me go," he answered. "I like this sort of life much better, and besides, no one gave me ice cream cones in the circus."

Well, pretty soon the rabbit and the elephant came to a place where there was a high mountain.

"Oh, we'll never get up that," said Uncle Wiggily.

"Yes, we will," said the elephant, "I'll make a hole through it with my tusks, and we can walk under it instead of climbing over."

So with his long, sharp tusks he made a tunnel right through the mountain, and, though it was a bit darkish, he and the rabbit went through it as easily as a mouse can nibble a bit of cheese.

Then, a little later they came to a place where there was a big river to cross, and there was no bridge.

"Oh, we can never get over that," said Uncle Wiggily.

"Yes, we can," said the elephant.

"Are you going to drink it up as you did the lake?" asked the rabbit.

"No," said the elephant, "but I will make a bridge to go over the river." So he found a great big tree that the wind had blown down, and, taking this in his strong trunk, the elephant laid it across the river, and then he laid another tree and another, and pretty soon he had as good a bridge as one could wish, and he and Uncle Wiggily crossed over on it.

Well, they hadn't gone on very far, before, all of a sudden the elephant fell down, and he was so heavy that he shook the ground just like when a locomotive choo-choo engine rushes past.

"Oh, whatever is the matter?" asked Uncle Wiggily. "Did you hurt yourself?"

"No," said the elephant, sad-like, "I am not hurt, but I am sick. I guess I drank too much ice water, which is a bad thing to do in hot weather. Oh, how ill I am! You had better go for a doctor."

Well, that poor elephant was so ill that he had to lie down on the ground, and he cried and groaned, and the big tears rolled down his trunk, and made quite a mud puddle on the earth. For when an elephant is ill he is very ill, indeed, as there is so much of him.

"I'll cover you with leaves so you won't get sunburned," said Uncle Wiggily, "and then I'll hop off for a doctor." Well, it takes a great number of leaves to cover up an elephant, but finally the rabbit did it, and then away he started.

He looked everywhere for an elephant doctor, but he couldn't seem to find any. There were dog doctors and horse doctors and cat doctors and even doctors for boys and girls, but none for the elephant.

"Oh, what shall I do?" thought the rabbit. "My poor, dear elephant may die."

Just then he heard some one singing in the woods like this:

"Peanuts, they are good to eat,
Mine are most especially neat,
I am going to make them hot
So that you will eat a lot."

"Oh, are you an elephant doctor?" cried Uncle Wiggily.

"No, I am a hot-peanut-man," said the voice, and then the

peanut roaster began to whistle like a tea kettle. "But, perhaps I can cure a sick elephant," said the peanut man. So he and Uncle Wiggily hurried off through the woods to where the elephant was groaning, and, would you believe it? as soon as the big chap heard the whistle of the hot-peanut wagon and smelled the nuts roasting he got well all of a sudden and he ate a bushel of the nuts and Uncle Wiggily had some also. So that's how the elephant got well, and he and the rabbit traveled on the next day.

UNCLE WIGGILY STARTS OFF

Uncle Wiggily Longears, the nice old gentleman rabbit, hopped out of bed one morning and started to go to the window, to see if the sun was shining. But, no sooner had he stepped on the floor, than he cried out:

"Oh! Ouch! Oh, dear me and a potato pancake! Oh, I believe I stepped on a tack! Sammie Littletail must have left it there! How careless of him!"

Well, when Uncle Wiggily felt that sharp pain, he stood still for a moment, and wondered what could have happened.

"Yes, I'm almost sure it was a tack," he said. "I must pick it up so no one else will step on it."

So Uncle Wiggily looked on the floor, but there was no tack there, only some crumbs from a sugar cookie that Susie Littletail had been eating the night before, when her uncle had told her a go-to-sleep story.

"Oh, I know what it was; it must have been my rheumatism that gave me the pain!" said the old gentleman rabbit as he looked for his red, white and blue crutch, striped like a barber pole. He found it under the bed, and then he managed to limp to the window. Surely enough, the sun was shining.

"I'll certainly have to do something about this rheumatism," said Uncle Wiggily as he carefully shaved himself by looking in the glass. "I guess I'll see Dr. Possum."

So after breakfast, when Sammie and Susie had gone to school, Dr. Possum was telephoned for, and he called to see Uncle Wiggily.

"Ha! Hum!" exclaimed the doctor, looking very wise. "You

have the rheumatism very bad, Mr. Longears."

"Why, I knew that before you came," said the old gentleman rabbit, blinking his eyes. "What I want is something to cure it."

"Ha! Hum!" said Dr. Possum, again looking very wise. "I think you need a change of air. You must travel about. Go on a journey, get out and see strange birds, and pick the pretty flowers. You don't get exercise enough."

"Exercise enough!" cried Uncle Wiggily. "Why, my goodness me sakes alive and a bunch of lilacs! Don't I play checkers almost every night with Grandfather Goosey Gander?"

"That is not enough," said the doctor, "you must travel here and there, and see things."

"Very well," said Uncle Wiggily, "then I will travel. I'll pack my valise at once, and I'll go off and seek my fortune, and maybe, on the way, I can lose this rheumatism."

So the next day Uncle Wiggily started out with his crutch, and his valise packed full of clean clothes, and something in it to eat.

"Oh, we are very sorry to have you go, dear uncle," said Susie Littletail, "but we hope you'll come back good and strong."

"Thank you," said Uncle Wiggily, as he kissed the two rabbit children and their mamma, and shook hands with Papa Littletail. Then off the old gentleman bunny hopped with his crutch.

Well, he went along for quite a distance, over the hills, and down the road, and through the woods, and, as the sun got higher and warmer, his rheumatism felt better.

"I do believe Dr. Possum was right!" said Uncle Wiggily. "Traveling is just the thing for me," and he felt so very jolly that he whistled a little tune about a peanut wagon, which roasted lemonade, and boiled and frizzled Easter eggs that Mrs. Cluk-Cluk laid.

"Ha! Where are you going?" suddenly asked a voice, as Uncle Wiggily finished the tune.

"I'm going to seek my fortune," replied Uncle Wiggily. "Who are you, pray?"

"Oh, I'm a friend of yours," said the voice, and Uncle Wiggily looked all around, but he couldn't discover any one.

"But where are you?" the puzzled old gentleman rabbit wanted to know. "I can't see you."

"No, and for a very good reason," answered the voice. "You see I have very weak eyes, and if I came out in the sun, without my smoked glasses on, I might get blind. So I have to hide down in this hollow stump."

"Then put on your glasses and come out where I can see you," invited the old gentleman rabbit, and all the while he was trying to remember where he had heard that voice before. At first he thought it might be Grandfather Goosey Gander, or Uncle Butter, the goat, yet it didn't sound like either of them.

"I have sent my glasses to the store to be fixed, so I can't wear them and come out," went on the voice. "But if you are seeking your fortune I know the very place where you can find it."

"Where?" asked Uncle Wiggily, eagerly.

"Right down in this hollow stump," was the reply. "There are all kinds of fortunes here, and you may take any kind you like Mr. Longears."

"Ha! That is very nice," thought the rabbit. "I have not had to travel far before finding my fortune. I wonder if there is a cure for rheumatism in that stump, too?" So he asked about it.

"Of course, your rheumatism can be cured in here," came the quick answer. "In fact, I guarantee to cure any disease—measles, chicken-pox, mumps and even toothache. So if you have any friends you want cured send them to me."

"I wish I could find out who you were," spoke the rabbit. "I seem to know your voice, but I can't think of your name."

"Oh, you'll know me as soon as you see me," said the voice. "Just hop down inside this hollow stump, and your fortune is as good as made, and your rheumatism will soon be gone. Hop right down."

Well, Uncle Wiggily didn't like the looks of the black hole down inside the stump, and he peered into it to see what he could see, but it was so black that all he could make out was something

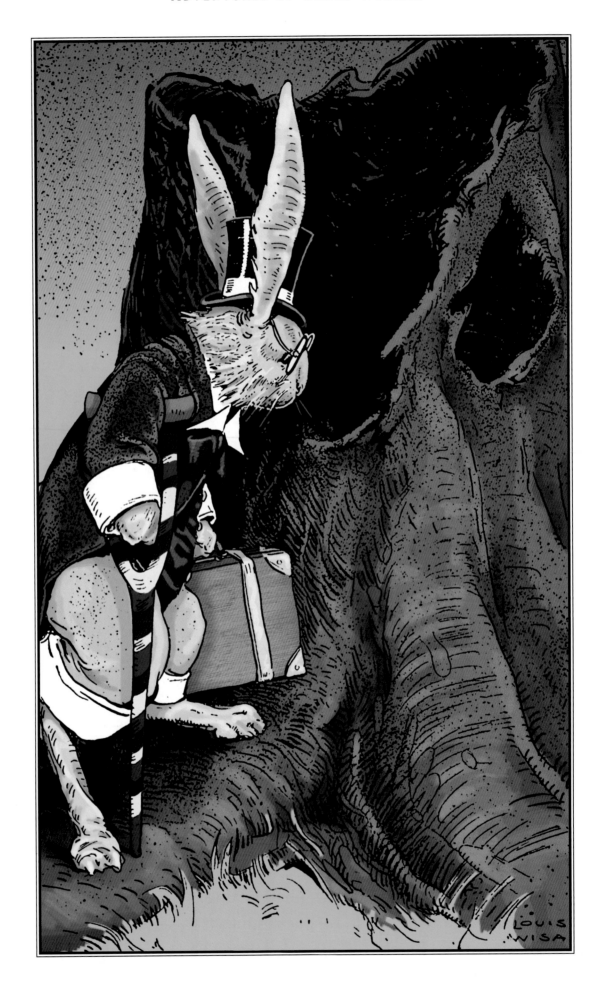

like a lump of coal.

"Well, Dr. Possum said I needed to have a change of scene, and some adventures," said the rabbit, "so I guess I'll chance it. I'll go down, and perhaps I may find my fortune."

Then, carefully holding his crutch and his satchel, Uncle Wiggily hopped down inside the stump. He felt something soft, and furry, and fuzzy, pressing close to him, and at first he thought he had bumped into Dottie or Willie Lambkin.

But then, all of a sudden, a harsh voice cried out:

"Ha! Now I have you! I was just wishing some one would come along with my dinner, and you did! Get in there, and see if you can find your fortune, Uncle Wiggily!" And with that what should happen but that big, black bear, who had been hiding in the stump, pushed Uncle Wiggily into a dark closet, and locked the door.

But don't worry! Uncle Wiggily found some rope that Sammie Littletail had put in his valise, and he used the rope to escape from the bear's closet. Lucky Uncle Wiggily!

UNCLE WIGGILY DOES SOME TRICKS

When two savage ducks—oh, I mean foxes—when two savage foxes jumped out of the bushes at Uncle Wiggily Longears and Fido Flip-Flop, the rabbit and the poodle doggie didn't know what in the world to do.

"Run this way!" called Fido, starting off to the left.

"No, hop this way!" said Uncle Wiggily, hopping to the right.

"Stand right where you are!" ordered the two foxes together. And with that one made a grab for Uncle Wiggily. But what did that brave rabbit gentleman do but stick his red-white-and-blue crutch out in front of him, and the fox bit on that instead of on Uncle Wiggily. Right into the crutch the fox's teeth sank, and for a moment Uncle Wiggily was safe. But not for long.

"Ah, you fooled me that time, but now I'll get you!" cried the fox, and, letting go of the crutch, he made another grab for the rabbit.

But at that instant Fido Flip-Flop, who had been jumping about, keeping out of the way of the fox that was after him, cried out quite loudly:

"Look here, everybody but Uncle Wiggily, and, as for you, shut both your eyes tight."

Now the old gentleman rabbit couldn't imagine why he was to shut his eyes tight, but he did so, and then what do you s'pose Fido Flip-Flop did? Why, he began turning somersaults so fast that he looked just like a pinwheel going around, or an automobile tire whizzing along. Faster and faster did Fido Flip-Flop turn around, and then, all of a sudden, he began chasing his tail, making motions just like a merry-go-round in a circus, until those two

foxes were fairly dizzy from watching him.

"Stop! Stop!" cried one fox.

"Yes do stop! We're so dizzy that we can't stand up!" cried the other fox, staggering about. "Stop!"

"No, I'll not!" answered Fido Flip-Flop, and he went around faster than ever, faster and faster and faster, until those two bad foxes got so dizzy-izzy that they fell right over on their backs, with their legs sticking straight up in the air like clothes posts, and their tails were wiggling back and forth in the dirt, like dusting brushes. Oh, but they were the dizzy foxes, though.

"Now's your chance! Run! Run! Uncle Wiggily! Run!" called Fido Flip-Flop. "Open your eyes and run!"

So the old gentleman rabbit opened his eyes, took up his valise which he had dropped, and, hopping on his crutch, he and the poodle doggie ran on through the woods, leaving the two surprised and disappointed foxes still lying on their backs, wiggling their tails in the dust, and too dizzy, from having watched Fido Flip-Flop do somersaults, and chase his tail, to be able to get up.

"Why did you want me to shut my eyes?" asked Uncle Wiggily, when they were so far away from the foxes that there was no more danger.

"That was so *you* wouldn't get dizzy from watching me do the flip-flops," answered the doggie. "My, but that was a narrow escape, though. Have you had many adventures like that since you started out to seek your fortune?"

"Yes, several," answered the rabbit. "But turning flip-flops is a very good thing to know how to do. I wonder if you could teach me, so that when any more foxes or alligators chase me I can make them dizzy by turning around? Can you teach me?"

"I'm sure I can," said Fido. "Here, this is the way to begin," and he did some flip-flops slow and easy-like. Then Uncle Wiggily tried them, and, though he couldn't do them very well at first, he practised until he was quite good at it. Then Fido showed him how to stand on one ear, and wiggle the other, and how to blink his eyes while standing on the end of his little tail, and then Uncle

Wiggily thought of a new trick, all by himself.

"I'll stick my crutch in the ground, like a clothes pole," he said to Fido, "and then I'll hop up on it and sing a song," which he did, singing a song that went like this:

"Did you ever see a rabbit
    Do a flipper-flopper-flap?
If not just kindly watch me,
    As I wear my baseball cap.

"It's very strange, some folks may say,
    And also rather funny,
To see a kinky poodle dog
    Play with a flip-flop bunny.

"But we are on our travels,
    Adventures for to seek,
We may find one, or two, or three,
    'Most any day next week."

And then Uncle Wiggily hopped down, and waved both ears backward and forward, and made a low bow to a make-believe crowd of people, only, of course, there were none there.

"Fine! Fine!" cried Fido Flip-Flop. "That's better than I did when I was in the circus. Now I'll tell you what let's do."

"What?" asked Uncle Wiggily.

"Let's go around and give little shows and entertainments, for little folks to see," went on the poodle doggie. "I can turn flip-flops, and you can stand on your head on your crutch, and sing a song, and then we'll take up a collection. I'll pass my hat, and perhaps we may make our fortune—who knows?"

"Who, indeed?" said Uncle Wiggily. "We'll do it."

So off they started together to give a little show, and make some money, and, as they went on through the woods, they practised doing the tricks Uncle Wiggily had learned.

Well, in a little while, not so very long, they came to a nice place in the forest—an open place where no trees grew.

"Here is a good spot for our show," said Uncle Wiggily.

"But there is no one to see us do the tricks," objected Fido.

"Oh, yes, there are some ants, and an angle worm, and a black bug and a grasshopper," said Uncle Wiggily. "They will do to start on, and after they see us do the tricks they'll tell other folks, and we'll have quite a crowd."

So they started in to do their tricks. Fido turned a lot of flip-flops, and Uncle Wiggily did a dance on the end of his crutch, and sang a song about a monkey-doodle, which the angle worm said was just fine, being quite cute, and the grasshopper made believe play a fiddle with his two hind legs, scratching one on the other, and making lovely music.

But, all of a sudden, just as Uncle Wiggily was standing on his left ear, and wiggling his feet in the air, which is a very hard trick for a rabbit, what should happen but that out of the woods sprang two boys.

"There's the dog! Grab him!" cried one boy. "Never mind about the rabbit! Get the trick dog!" And the boys rushed right up, knocking Uncle Wiggily down, and grabbing Fido Flip-Flop. And they started off through the woods with him, while Uncle Wiggily cried out for them to come back. But they wouldn't.

UNCLE WIGGILY AND THE DOG

Uncle Wiggily's rheumatism was quite bad after he got wet in a fountain, and when he thanked a mamma cat-bird and her kitten-birds for saving him, he found that he could hardly walk, much less carry his heavy valise.

"Oh, we'll help you," said Mrs. Cat-Bird. "Here, Flitter and Flutter, you carry the satchel for Uncle Wiggily, and we'll take him to our house."

"But, mamma," said Flutter, who was getting to be quite a big bird-boy, "Uncle Wiggily can't climb up a tree to our nest."

"No, but we can make him a nice warm bed on the ground," said the mamma bird. "So you and Flitter carry the satchel. Put a long blade of grass through the handle, and then each of you take hold of one end of the grass in your bills, and fly away with it. Skimmer, you and Dartie go on ahead, and get something ready to eat, and I'll show Uncle Wiggily the way."

So Flitter and Flutter, the two boy birds, flew away with the satchel, and Skimmer and Dartie, the girl birds, flew on ahead to set the table, and put on the teakettle on the stove to boil, and Mrs. Cat-Bird flew slowly on over Uncle Wiggily, to show him the way.

Well, pretty soon, not so so very long, they came to where the birds lived. And those good children had already started to make a nest on the ground for the old gentleman rabbit. They had it almost finished, and by the time supper was ready it was all done. Then came the meal, and those birds couldn't do enough for Uncle Wiggily, because they liked him so.

When it got dark, they covered him all up, with soft leaves in the nest on the ground, and there he slept until morning. His rheumatism wasn't quite so bad when, after breakfast, he had sat out in the warm sun for a while, and after a bit he said:

"Well, I think I'll travel along now, and see if I can find my fortune to-day. Perhaps I may, and if I do I'll come back and bring you more peanuts."

"Oh, that'll be fine and dandy!" cried Flitter and Flutter, and Skimmer and Dartie. So they said good-by to the old gentleman rabbit, and once more he started off.

"My! I'm certainly getting to be a great traveler," he thought as he walked along through the woods and over the fields. "But I don't ever seem to get to any place. Something always happens to me. I hope everything goes along nicely to-day."

But you just wait and see what takes place. I'm afraid something is going to happen very shortly, but it's not my fault, and all I can do is to tell you exactly all about it. Wait! There, it's beginning to happen now.

All of a sudden, as Uncle Wiggily was traveling along, he came to a place in the woods where a whole lot of Gypsies had their wagons and tents. And on one tent, in which was an old brown and wrinkled Gypsy lady, there was a sign which read:

FORTUNES TOLD HERE.

"Ha! If they tell fortunes in that tent, perhaps the Gypsy lady can tell me where to find mine," thought Uncle Wiggily. "I'll go up and ask her."

Well, he was just going to the tent when he happened to think that perhaps the Gypsy woman wouldn't understand rabbit talk. So he sat there in the bushes thinking what he had better do, when all at once, before he could wiggle his ears more than four times, a great big, bad, ugly dog sprang at him, barking, oh! so loudly.

"Come on, Browser!" cried this dog to another one. "Here is a fat rabbit that we can catch for dinner. Come on, let's chase him!"

Well, you can just imagine how frightened Uncle Wiggily was.

He didn't sit there, waiting for that dog to catch him, either. No, indeed, and a bag of popcorn besides! Up jumped Uncle Wiggily, with his crutch and his valise, and he hopped as hard and as fast as he could run. My! How his legs did twist in and out.

"Come on! Come!" barked the first dog to the second one.

"I'm coming! I'm coming! Woof! Woof! Bow-w-w Bow-wow!" barked the second dog.

Poor Uncle Wiggily's heart beat faster and faster, and he didn't know which way to run. Every way he turned the dogs were after him, and soon more of the savage animals came to join the first two, until all the dogs in that Gypsy camp were chasing the poor old gentleman rabbit.

"I guess I'll have to drop my satchel or my crutch," thought Uncle Wiggily. "I can't carry them much farther. Still, I don't want to lose them." So he held on to them a little longer, took a good breath and ran on some more.

He thought he saw a chance to escape by running across in front of the fortune-telling tent, and he started that way, but a Gypsy man, with a gun, saw him and fired at him. I'm glad to say, however, that he didn't shoot Uncle Wiggily, or else I couldn't tell any more stories about him.

Uncle Wiggily got safely past the tent, but the dogs were almost up to him now. One of them was just going to catch him by his left hind leg, when one of the Gypsy men cried out:

"Grab him, Biter! Grab him! We'll have rabbit potpie for dinner; that's what we'll have!"

Wasn't that a perfectly dreadful way to talk about our Uncle Wiggily? But just wait, if you please.

Biter, the bad dog, was just going to grab the rabbit, when all of a sudden, Uncle Wiggily saw a big hole in the ground.

"That's what I'm looking for!" he exclaimed. "I'm going down there, and hide away from these dogs!"

So into the hole he popped, valise, crutch and all, and oh! how glad he was to get into the cool, quiet darkness, leaving those savage, barking dogs outside. But wait a moment longer, if you please.

Biter and Browser stopped short at the hole.

"He's gone—gotten clean away!" exclaimed Browser. "Isn't that too bad?"

"No, we'll get him yet!" cried Biter. "Here, you watch at this hole, while I go get a pail of water. We'll pour the water down, under the ground where the rabbit is, and that will make him come out, and we'll eat him."

"Good!" cried Browser. So while he stood there and watched, Biter went for the water. But, mind you, Uncle Wiggily had sharp ears and he heard what they were saying, and what do you think he did?

Why, with his sharp claws he went right to work, and he dug, and dug, and dug in the back part of that underground place, until he had made another hole, far off from the first one, and he crawled out of that, with his crutch and valise, just as Biter was pouring the water down the first hole.

"Ah, ha! I think this will astonish those dogs!" thought Uncle Wiggily, and he took a peep at them from behind a bush where they couldn't see him, and then he hopped on through the woods, to look for more adventures, leaving the dogs still pouring water.

UNCLE WIGGILY AND PERCIVAL

Now I'm going to tell you, before I forget it, why old dog Percival was crying one time when he came to a little stone house where the hedgehog lived, and where Uncle Wiggily gave him some cherry pie. And the reason Percival was crying, was because he had stepped on a sharp stone, and hurt his foot.

"But I don't in the least mind now," said Percival, after he had eaten about sixty-'leven pieces of the pie. "My foot is all better."

"I should think that cherry pie would make almost any one better," said the hedgehog, laughing with joy, for he felt better, too. "I know some bad boys to whom I'm going to give some cherry pie, and I hope it makes them better. And to think I threw away the good part of the cherries and cooked the stones in the pie. Oh, excuse me while I laugh again!"

And the hedgehog laughed so hard that he spilled some of the red cherry pie juice on his shirt front, but he didn't care, for he had another shirt.

Well, Uncle Wiggily and Percival, the old circus dog, stayed for some days at the home of the hedgehog, and they had cherry pie, or fritters with maple syrup, at almost every meal. Then, finally, Uncle Wiggily said:

"Well, I guess I must travel on. I can't find my fortune here. I must start off to-morrow."

"And I'll go with you," spoke Percival. "We'll go together, and see what we can find."

Well, he and Uncle Wiggily went on together for some time, and nothing happened, except that they met a poor pussy cat without any tail, and Uncle Wiggily gave her some of the pie. And the next day they met a cat and seven little kittens, and they all had tails, so they had to have some pie, too.

But one night, after Percival and Uncle Wiggily had been traveling all day, they came to a deep, dark, dismal woods.

"Oh, have we got to go through that forest?" asked the old gentleman rabbit, wrinkling up his ears—I mean his nose.

"I guess we have," replied the circus dog. "We may find our fortunes in there."

"It is a pretty dark spot to look for money, or fortunes," said the rabbit. "The best thing we can do is to look for a place to sleep, and in the morning we will hurry out of the woods."

Well, the two animal friends started into the grove of trees, and they hadn't gone very far before it got so dark that they couldn't see to go any farther. Oh, but it was black and lonesome and sort of scary-like! and Uncle Wiggily said:

"Let's stay here, Percival. We'll make a little bed under the trees to sleep in, and we'll build a fire to keep us warm, and cook a little supper."

So Percival thought that would be nice, and soon he and the rabbit had a cheerful little fire blazing, and then it wasn't quite so lonely. Only there was a big owl in a tree, and he kept hollering "Who? Who? Who?" and Percival thought it meant him, and Uncle Wiggily thought it meant him, and they were rather frightened, so they didn't either of them answer the owl, who kept on calling "Who? Who? Who?"

They were just cooking their supper, and cutting up the cherry pie, and putting it on some oak leaves for plates, and they had picked out a nice smooth stump for a table, when, all of a sudden, they heard a voice saying:

"Now you make a jump and grab the rabbit and I'll take the dog. Then we can carry them off to our dens, and that will be the last of them. Get ready now!"

"Did you hear that?" asked Uncle Wiggily of the circus dog.

"Indeed I did," replied Percival. "I wonder if it can be those owls?"

"It doesn't sound like them," said Uncle Wiggily. "I think it is a bad fox, or maybe two of them."

And just then they looked off through the woods, and by the light of the fire they saw two big, savage, ugly wolves. Oh, how their sharp teeth gleamed in the dancing flames, and how red their tongues were!

"Come on! Grab 'em both!" cried one savage wolf. "Grab the rabbit and the dog!"

"Sure! I'm with you!" growled the other savage wolf.

"Oh, what shall we do, Uncle Wiggily?" asked Percival. "They'll eat us up!"

"Let me think a minute," said the rabbit. So he thought for maybe half a minute, and then exclaimed: "Oh! I know a good thing to do."

"What?" asked Percival. "Say it quickly, Uncle Wiggily, for those wolves are creeping up on us, and it's so dark we can't see to run away."

And surely enough, those wolves were sneaking up, with their red tongues hanging out longer than ever, for all the world just as if they had eaten cherry pie.

"We must do some funny tricks!" exclaimed Uncle Wiggily. "You know how, Percival, for you were once in a circus, and I learned some when I was with the monkey, and with Fido Flip-Flop. Do some tricks, and maybe these wolves will feel so good-natured that they won't bite us."

So brave Uncle Wiggily stood up on one ear and waved his feet in the air. Then he stood on his nose and turned a somersault. Next he went around and around as fast as a pinwheel, and he whistled a funny tune about a little rubber ball that flew into the air, and when it landed on the ground it would not stay down there.

But I wish you could have seen the tricks Percival did. He jumped through between Uncle Wiggily's long ears, and he walked on his hind legs, and on his front ones. Then he stood on his head, and he made believe he was begging for something to eat, and

Uncle Wiggily fed him a carrot, and a piece of pie. Then he put a piece of bread on his nose, tossed it up into the air—tossed the bread, I mean, not his nose—and when it came down he caught it and ate it. Oh, it was great!

Well, those wolves were too surprised for anything. They had never seen tricks like those. First they smiled a bit. Then they smiled some more. Then one laughed, then the other laughed, and finally, when Uncle Wiggily and Percival took turns jumping over each other's backs, the wolves thought it so funny that they had to lie down on the leaves and roll over and over because they were laughing so hard.

And, of course, after that they didn't feel like hurting Uncle Wiggily or Percival. And just then the big alligator came along and chased the wolves away, so the rabbit and dog had no one to bother them except the alligator, and, as he had just had his supper, he wasn't hungry, so he didn't eat them.

So Uncle Wiggily and Percival went to sleep, and so must you.